T15i

IT
HAPPENED
AT
CECILIA'S

IT HAPPENED AT CECILIA'S

ERIKA TAMAR

Atheneum
1989
NEW YORK

Atheneum
Macmillan Publishing Company
866 Third Avenue, New York, NY 10022
Collier Macmillan Canada, Inc.
First Edition   Printed in the United States of America

10 9 8 7 6 5 4 3 2 1

Library of Congress Cataloging-in-Publication Data
Tamar, Erika.
It happened at Cecilia's.
Summary: Ninth-grader Andy's relatively stable life
with his father and his cat living above their Manhattan
restaurant is threatened when his father falls in love
and their restaurant is discovered by a restaurant critic,
bringing the Mafia in for a cut of the increasing business.
[1. Single-parent family—Fiction.   2. Restaurants,
lunch rooms, etc.—Fiction.   3. Cats—Fiction]   I. Title
PZ7.T159It 1989   [Fic]   88-28502
ISBN 0–689–31478–7

To Bunny Gabel—thank you

Acknowledgments

Special thanks to Monica Sapirstein for zany restaurant stories and to Ray Sapirstein for much of chapter 8.

IT HAPPENED AT CECILIA'S

1

I'M TRYING TO DECIDE ON MY ESCAPE ROUTE OUT OF school. Getting beat up is not my idea of a great afternoon. The front way, down the main stairs, would be the logical way to go, but there's a little side exit near the gym and I could slip out that way pretty easily. I'm walking with Jo-Jo and Garrity and some of the other guys, though, and I'd have to give them some sort of reason for going off by myself. And I don't feel like talking about my problem.

I have a problem, all right, and his name is Donald "Bear" Abbott. You might say Bear Abbott is my nemesis.

> *nemesis* n pl-ses 1 a: just punishment b: one who imposes it 2: anyone or anything that seems inevitably to defeat or frustrate one

We'd better zero in on the second meaning. He imposes punishment, but I wouldn't say it's just. He does inevitably defeat me.

That's a strong word for ninth-grade vocabulary. Ms. Morfly takes special pleasure in piling the tough ones on me. What she doesn't know is that I like oddball words. I like to wrap my tongue around *nemesis, miasma, pandemonium,* and *paroxysm* and slip them into conversation now and then. Morfly says I have a mouth, but I don't think she's talking about my vocabulary.

Sometimes just the sound of words has an effect. The stand-up comic who comes into Cecilia's says that words with *p* and *k* sounds in them make people laugh. Paducah and Pocatello are funny; Trenton isn't. A line with lots of *p*'s and *k*'s in it leads to a paroxysm of laughter.

Morfly never laughs. She's dried-up and boring, and it's kind of fun to get her flustered. Her eyes dart all over the place and her lips get compressed into this tight line. Like when she caught Jo-Jo passing notes and yelled at him.

Jo-Jo did his persecuted indignant look and whined, "How come you're always picking on the poor black kid?"

Everybody cracked up, because Jo-Jo's dad is a big-time architect and he's a very popular kid, a monster at soccer. At games, everybody's always yelling, "Go, Joe! Joe! Joe!" That's how he became Jo-Jo. But Morfly turned red and her lips clamped down so hard you'd think they'd be locked forever.

So a few days later, when she caught me horsing around and made me stand up, I couldn't resist.

"How come you're always picking on the poor motherless child?"

Miscalculation. Nobody laughed. I guess "motherless" cuts too close, fear of abandonment and all that. Look, I can't miss someone I don't even remember. Oh well, even the best bomb sometimes.

She went around the room, asking everyone the answer to some arcane grammatical point. "I don't know." "I don't know." A veritable chorus of "I don't knows," so when she got to me, I thought I'd try for variety.

"This is a miasma of confusion, Ms. Morfly."

"You've got a mouth, Andrew Szabo." The unexpected makes Morfly angry.

I kind of liked that, so I bill myself as Andy "The Mouth" Szabo. All the in kids have nicknames. There's Jo-Jo and "Orange" Garrity. His mom was hanging on as an over-the-hill flower child when he was born, so she named him "Sun-kissed." Legally, honest to God. Can you picture a guy going through life as "Sun-kissed Garrity"? We did him a big favor by dubbing him "Orange." And then there's Bear Abbott. He's not in my class, but in his case I doubt the nickname denotes affection. It sure fits, though. Bear. He's a mammoth kid with a bullet-shaped head and this lumbering bearlike way of walking. Bear Abbott, my nemesis.

He's not what you would call a gentle giant. The problem started in the lunchroom one day. The cafeteria is always jammed, two pounds of kids in a one-pound sack. Then there's the noise level, with the lunchroom aides screaming "Quiet!" louder than anyone, and the stale egg smells and the damp metal tables. Dad says ambiance is very important. Cecilia's—that's the restaurant Dad and Cajun Jack own, Cecilia's in Greenwich Village—has one terrific ambiance, something the cafeteria sorely lacks. So at least I draw the line at cardboard food and I usually bring lunch from home. Cajun Jack packs something left over from the night before or something that he's preparing early for the lunch shift. On that particular day, I came into the lunch room late (trouble with Morfly—she kept me after class). All my favorite tables were filled, so I sat down where Bear was. I opened up the brown paper bag and was happy to find French bread and a container of ratatouille. It's one of those things that's even better the next day, when all the flavors have a chance to kind of blend. I was savoring it and anticipating the eclair coming up and generally minding my own business.

"Hey, kid, what's that you're eating?" Bear said.

"Ratatouille," I said.

"Rat—a what?" he said in his Neanderthal way.

"Ratatouille," I said patiently. "A stew of eggplant, tomato, green pepper, zucchini, and—"

"Looks more like rat turds to me."

I could have ignored him and finished fast and maybe that would have been the end of it. I could have, but I didn't. What flashed in my mind was the loving care Cajun Jack puts into it, so the mouth took over.

"A damn lot better than the morass of slime you've got there," I said.

"Oh, yeah? Well, try it, turkey." He threw the remains of his macaroni and cheese at me, plate and all. I ducked to the side and it landed on a lunchroom aide's rolled-up stocking.

"Great throw, pinhead," I said. My hand wrapped itself around the eclair. "Have some dessert!" It was a beautiful landing, smack on his forehead, custard cream gently oozing down his nose.

"Food fight! Food fight!" The cry went up and, needless to say, it was pandemonium. It was kind of funny. Unfortunately, Bear seemed to lack a sense of humor. It took two lunchroom aides to hold him back. "You're dead," he muttered.

Well, the afternoon droned on and I forgot about it, except for a faint tinge of regret at the wasted eclair —baked on the premises at Cecilia's, none of that outside prepackaged pastry most restaurants have. After school I innocently went out the door and Bear was waiting for me.

I didn't have a chance. My friends were no help either. They stood around, holding my books, looking worried—but this was one-on-one. I tried to land a punch—or at least protect myself—but Bear has it all over me in size and weight. His fist alone was the size of a side of beef and it kept coming at me. *Smash* in my nose, *smash* in my gut, the air knocked out of me and *pain*. You see a Technicolor TV fight with lots of grunts, but you forget about anyone hurting. Well, this was real, me tasting blood, my nose filling up with it, pain radiating across my cheekbones, my mouth turning numb, pain scrunching my ribs. Finally Bear had enough, for that day anyway.

Well, I wasn't dead and though I looked like hell for a while, there wasn't permanent damage—but remembering the way it felt still makes me wince. I had to cancel my Sunday visit with my Grandma Van Dorn—the way I looked would just add ammunition to her conviction that I'm being raised wrong, "by an irresponsible egomaniac and a convict to boot," unquote, meaning my dad and Cajun Jack. It's awful to have her hate Dad so much.

Anyway—I thought, okay, it was done with, but then about a week later, Bear caught me again, just past the main exit, right in the middle of the stream of kids leaving school. This time, it was out of the blue, no eclairs thrown, no words exchanged. I figure Bear had so much fun, he was going to make a habit of it.

Enumerating all the details would get boring. There was a bit of variation—a blackened left eye instead of the right, a kick in the groin, a cut lip—and then Bear, his bloodlust momentarily satisfied, sneering "until next time, kid," playing to an audience of half the school. It dawned on me that this was going to be his regular form of recreation.

So I've been sneaking around trying to avoid him. I see him in the halls at school when classes change, but he can't do much there. "Later," he mutters, just loud enough to let everyone hear his tough-guy routine. Seems like every time he spots me, especially when there's a good audience, it triggers something in his minuscule brain. I've been dashing out the side exits and going home the long way around to avoid MacDougal Street, which is Bear territory, and I don't even ride my bike down by the piers with Jo-Jo and Garrity anymore, 'cause that's where Bear hangs out. I hate the way I feel, small and squirmy and ashamed. I'd rather be a hero. But that's not the way it is. Bear is six foot two and weighs around two hundred, and there's nothing I know to do except try to stay alive.

I'm being honest, humiliation and all, because of Mrs. Johnson. She was my eighth-grade English teacher in the good old pre-Morfly days. She was great and treated kids like real people; most teachers say outrageous things they wouldn't dare spring on an adult. I told her I might want to be a writer and I even showed her the beginning of a screenplay that I thought was pretty good. It was about this cool guy who solves a murder in this South American nightclub with a one-way see-through mirror, and there's a safe with a coded combination where they keep the heist of emeralds that have an old Inca curse on them. . . . Mrs. Johnson said it was fun, but there were two things I should do, at least to start off—write about what I know and try to tell the truth about it.

What I know is my own turf, Greenwich Village, down to every last cobblestone on Bank Street. Sticking to the truth is the hard part. I think it would make a better story if Cajun Jack quick, overnight, taught me to box and then Bear, dumbfounded with surprise at my great uppercut, was demolished once and for all. Or if I took lessons and became a black belt in record time—Andy "Karate Kid" Szabo!—and my superpower kick destroyed Bear in front of the whole ninth grade . . . Actually, I don't know what's going to happen.

A writer's supposed to think about what makes people tick. I'm supposed to wonder if Bear gets abused at home or got dropped on his head when he was a baby or if he's just a natural psychopath. To tell the truth, I couldn't care less. I wish the earth would open up and swallow him.

The first time Bear creamed me, I went through the kitchen when I came home so my dad wouldn't see the worst of it. Dad has these very expressive dark eyes. His feelings show all the time, he holds nothing back, and I knew he'd be feeling the pain for me, worse than I did. My dad, Lazlo Szabo—he came over right after the Hungarian revolution. He was just a little baby then, but I keep imagining him throwing rocks at tanks and the hell with the consequences. That's the way he is—all emotion and action. I can't picture him running away from anything.

I avoided the front of the restaurant and came in through the kitchen, where Cajun Jack was. He's big and calm and he cleaned up my wounds, completely deadpan, no questions asked. Grandma Van Dorn is right about him being an ex-con. He served time for manslaughter. It was a barroom brawl and he'd been drinking and it involved a woman he was in love with and another guy. That's all I know. He won't say anything about it. We're real close, but that subject is taboo. He doesn't drink at all anymore and he's this big, tough-looking dude who tries to steer clear of trouble. Even when he has to bounce someone at Cecilia's, he tries to *talk* them out.

"What do you do when someone twice your size is after you?"

He thought about it. "He's twice your size, that one?"

"Yeah." I winced as he cleaned up the scrape on my cheekbone.

"Me, I'd defend myself."

"I tried. It was like a fly one-on-one with a rhinoceros."

"So then you try to get away or else take it."

I nodded. There weren't any terrific choices.

His hand was on my shoulder and he gave it a squeeze. That's about as emotional as Cajun Jack gets, but I know he would do anything for me. There was nothing I could ask him to do, though.

Later, I came out to the front, looking a little better but with my eye turning colors and my nose swelling fast. Dad was at the bar, talking to two of the regulars. His reaction was predictable.

"Who did that to you?"

I told him. I was dying with embarrassment.

"Show me that sonofabitch! I'll tear him apart! I'll rip him to pieces!"

"Hey, Lazlo, you can't mix in a schoolkids' fight." That was Mason; he comes into Cecilia's in the afternoons. You can tell he's an artist by the green paint under his fingernails.

"Then listen, Andy," Dad said. "He bothers you again, you give him one punch, one punch he'll remember. Make it cost him in pain and he'll steer clear."

"Sure, Dad," I said.

"Lazlo, if this guy's as big as Andy says . . ." That was the other regular. I hated turning it into a public discussion.

"Then do whatever you have to. Come up behind him with a baseball bat. Kick him where it hurts. Gouge out his eyes. . . ."

Mason shook his head and laughed. Dad was grasping at straws. I hated seeing the hurt look in his eyes; they were almost welling up.

"It's okay, Dad," I said. "It's over."

Sure it was. That's why I'm not walking home with Jo-Jo and Orange Garrity and sneaking around and almost sighing with relief when I finally get to the red-and-white striped awning of Cecilia's.

2

I LIKE COMING HOME OUT OF THE COLD TO THE LATE afternoon hush at Cecilia's. We don't start serving dinner until six, so no customers are in yet. The tables are set up already, starchy white tablecloths and red paper napkins and a bud vase with a single red zinnia on each one. It's not a big place, eight tables for four plus some small ones on the side and then the bar on the other side, but it sure looks nice. All that starchy white against the dark wood walls—Dad says it's worth it to splurge on tablecloths.

The laundry bills are high, though, especially with the new laundry service. I remember when the guy from the new service came in the first time—a spiffy dresser with a wide, flat face and a dead look about his eyes. He and Dad talked for a long time, looked like they were arguing, and then Cajun Jack joined them and they argued some more. I don't know why Dad wound up switching—it's twice as much. Maybe they use more starch or something. Dad's a perfectionist about ambiance. Anyway, he's cutting costs by putting zinnias in the vases instead of roses.

The rich smell of paprika hits me as soon as I come through the door and makes my mouth water. Most people don't even know what real Hungarian paprika smells like until they come to Cecilia's. That stuff in little tin cans that you see at the supermarket is food coloring, that's all. Dad gets the real McCoy, imported, both medium and hot, which makes a good blend. Three-meat goulash and chicken paprikasch are staples on our menu, along with Cajun Jack's Hoppin' John jambalaya. Mellow lighting and mouth-watering smells and the expectant hush.

Maggie's at the cash register, her hips overflowing her chair. She's kind of slow—her lips move when she counts—but she's a failed sculptress (I guess that's why she has massive arms) and needed the job. Anyway, she's been with us since the beginning.

"Hey, Maggie."

"Hi. How's it going?"

"Okay. Where's my dad?"

"He went upstairs for a little shut-eye."

Our apartment is right above the restaurant. This is the slowest part of the day and sometimes Dad takes a catnap. He's up at dawn at the markets and then, after dinner service, the bar crowd comes in. He doesn't quit until the early hours.

Katie is curled up on the end of the bar. She's the prettiest tabby you'll ever see, gray and black stripes on top, tan underneath, a white chin, long whiskers, everything perfectly symmetrical. I scratch behind her ears and she looks up at me appreciatively, her head tilted back, giving me a pussycat smile.

"That cat doesn't belong there," Maggie says.

"She'll go when it gets busy," I say. The bar is the perfect vantage point for her to observe the room. She'll retreat under a table or into the kitchen when the bar crowd comes in. Katie hates the smell of smoke and liquor.

Bob, our bartender, hasn't come in yet. When he's late, it's usually because he got held up at an audition. He's a failed actor; he hasn't had an acting job in the last five years. Bob doesn't get along with D.K., who does kitchen prep. Before the customers come in, D.K. plays rock from a Chinese station full blast on his radio and sings along off key at top voice. It makes Bob nervous because he likes to meditate before we open for business; he says that helps his concentration as an actor. D.K. and Bob haven't really had words because D.K. doesn't speak English. Actually, D.K. has everybody cowed because he's very temperamental and runs the kitchen with an iron fist. He has a snake tattooed on his arm; its tail wiggles as his muscles move when he's chopping something.

Ellen, the night waitress, should be along pretty soon. She's gorgeous, long curly blond hair and big eyes framed with purple mascara and a great bod that makes my bone marrow melt. She's even come into my dreams at night a couple of times. Sometimes she runs her fingers through my hair and teases me about wavy locks and I worry that a certain inappropriate swelling is going to show. She thinks I'm just a kid. She's an NYU student and a failed waitress. Dizzy, gets orders mixed up and forgets things, but she's real perky, and Dad says the customers like her. Anyway, this is a very casual place—except for the food.

I sit down on a bar stool and slowly scratch Katie's neck and rub my nose against the silky fur on her side. She rolls over on her back and ecstatically offers her tummy, her front paws held aloft. I swivel around and lean against the bar. A shaft of pale November sunshine is coming through the front window and forms a light band of dancing dust motes.

There are paintings all over the walls and they've been there so long that I mostly don't see them. Some are Dad's: oils, vivid slashes of reds, yellows, violets, thick paint textured with knife strokes, "Lazlo Szabo" bold in the corners. Most are my mother's: watercolors, delicate shades, intricate details, with her name in a small, neat hand—"Cecilia Van Dorn" on some and "Cecilia Szabo" on others. I don't know enough to tell if they're any good; my mother's look like they took more work. Dad says she died too young to be recognized. I wonder what she was like. Dad gets a hurt, soft look in his eyes when he talks about her. Cecilia's is kind of a shrine—her name over the door, her paintings all over the walls.

I guess he really loves the restaurant because he finally found his true calling. Dad was in art school when he met Cecilia; by the time I was born, he was trying to make it as a painter and not doing real well. My Grandma Van Dorn could have helped out, but she didn't because she was dead set against them getting married in the first place. Anyway, Dad was home a lot, and their friends, mostly poor artists, used to drop in and he'd cook up a pot of goulash and little dumplings—that's his soul food—and feed everybody. He says if it's true that you are what you eat, then serving good honest food to your friends is the ultimate gift. He loves to take care of everyone—he was the one who picked up Katie on the street last year when she was a starving, flea-covered kitten—and so he'd make different dishes and there was always a crowd around at mealtimes.

Then he ran into Cajun Jack and they were the perfect combination. Cajun Jack had some money and was thinking about opening a restaurant, but an ex-con can't get a liquor license. Dad had no money at all, but he had a big following and a clean record, because that's the kind of nice guy he is. Cecilia's was born and somehow chicken paprikasch and pecan pie and crayfish gumbo and Dobos torte worked out fine. My mother used to be at the cash register until Maggie had to take over.

A lot of the artists Dad knew live in Alphabet City now, from Avenue A all the way east to Avenue D, because Village rents are too high, but they still come in all the time, along with the comics who work the club across the street. It's mostly regulars, and Dad says where else could a guy make a living hanging out with his friends and doing what he likes. It's a real labor of love. You should see him at the markets—looking for new kinds of lettuce, checking the gills on the fish, finding the freshest stuff. I only went with him a couple of times; I'm not into getting up when it's still dark.

"Andy!" It's Dad's voice and I whirl around on the stool.

"Hi, Dad."

He just came down from the apartment and he comes over and gives me a big hug—I'm glad no one's around to see.

"How was school today?"

"Fine."

"Any more trouble from that kid?"

"No," I say.

He goes behind the bar and starts polishing glasses. When Bob is late, Dad tends bar.

"So it's all blown over?"

"Yeah," I lie.

He looks up at me and smiles. "Okay, that's good."

Ellen comes drifting in and puts on the red Cecilia's apron. After a while the first couple of customers sit down at a back table and then Herb Lee comes in. He usually eats real early, so his stomach will be settled before it's show time across the street. I hear he throws up a lot, anyway. They feature new, young comics—only Herb's not so new or young anymore.

"Lazlo, my man. What's happening?"

Dad pushes a shot of Scotch across the bar. "Not much. Thursday night's dead."

Herb downs the shot and grimaces. "You're telling me. Thursday night audience, man, they scrape the pits for Thursday night." He moves to a side table and I hear him saying something to Ellen and Ellen's laughing.

He's one of the funniest men alive, *after* a show, when it's all over and he's relaxed. I love it when all the comics hang out at the bar, just bopping, trying out new material, improvising, topping each other. I stick around to listen—until Dad remembers to ship me up to bed. I swear, it's better than any TV show. And Herb is the best, just pulling things out of the air. He did fifteen minutes once on Dad's birthplace, Budapest, which is really two places—Buda and Pest—and he carried it into this wild monologue on pest control that had me laughing until my sides hurt.

The trouble is, he tries too hard in front of a paying audience. I saw him one time, on this dinky little stage, running around like a demented chicken, with half his stuff falling flat. He was dying, you could see him sweat, and he kept getting louder and louder.

Dad sees me watching him with Ellen and follows my train of thought. "Andy, that's one of the bravest men I know."

"Bravest or craziest," I say.

"He goes out there and faces it every night. I respect bravery," Dad says.

I think about me and Bear, and I shrink inside.

Ellen is bringing cucumber salad to the couple at table three and that reminds me I'm starving. I'm about to go back to the kitchen to see what Cajun Jack's got for me when the front door opens again.

A slim woman in her twenties hesitantly comes in, clutching a threadbare coat around her. Long, mousy-color hair, mousy-color coat, a dead-white face.

"Excuse me," she says in a wispy voice. "Is there a telephone I could—"

Maggie starts to answer when the woman reaches out for a chair, misses it, and sags down to the floor.

Maggie comes around the cash register, Ellen stands and stares, and Dad whips over from the bar and picks her up.

He stands there, holding her, and her eyelids start to flutter. "Oh," she says. "I'm sorry—I—"

There's a beat, and he's looking at her.

"I'm sorry," she says. "I don't know what happened. . . . I'm all right. . . ."

He's still holding her. "You weigh less than a feather."

"I didn't eat today and I guess I—I—"

Magic words to set Dad into action. The next thing you know, he's got her at a table.

"Ellen, get a bowl of gumbo and some French bread."

"Oh no, please, I can't pay for—I was just going to use the phone and—"

"Hey, it's all right," Dad says.

What's all right? Cecilia's can't operate on free lunch!

Ellen comes back with the soup and then Dad is watching her eat with this look on his face, like her faint is the greatest thing he's seen all day.

Between spoonfuls, we hear her story. Her name is Lorraine and she's a dancer, but she's been out of work for a while and she's been running to auditions all week and then her money was stolen and she's out of cash and (with a sob in her voice, the greatest tragedy of all) she can't even afford her daily dance class anymore! And she was just going to phone her family, collect, back in Des Moines, to wire train fare home, she can't make it in New York, it's too hard, she's giving up— As she talks and eats, she starts to look better in a pale kind of way. We're all crowding around, listening, but her eyes are on Dad the whole time. She plays with the napkin. "Thank you," she says, in a breathless voice reserved for one's savior.

As hard-luck stories go, it's not that interesting— but Dad is listening, fascinated. I guess she has kind of pretty eyes, green-flecked hazel, but still— The next thing you know, he's telling her not to give up—she can help Maggie at the register. . . .

"I don't need help," Maggie says, miffed.

"You know we're shorthanded when it's busy. There's lots of odds and ends she can do," Dad says. I assume he didn't offer Ellen's territory because Lorraine doesn't look strong enough to lift a plate.

Maggie opens her mouth to object, but Dad gives her a fierce look that stops her cold.

"I've been thinking of hiring someone," Dad says. "You walked in at just the right time."

"Do you really think so?" she says in a whisper.

They're transfixed by each other's eyes and I expect the violins to start any minute. I know Dad has an eye for the ladies, but this is ridiculous. Somehow, I'd like her to hightail it right back to Des Moines.

3

THERE'S SOMETHING I FIGURED OUT ABOUT BEAR ABbott. He likes an audience. When no one else is in the school halls, he'll pass by me without saying anything. As soon as there's a bunch of people around, the muttered threats start. I guess he's using me to beef up his image. It's hell on my image, though.

I don't like thinking about Bear. I'd rather have Kim O'Hara on my mind.

Kim O'Hara is in my French class and I've been watching her all term. She's half-Chinese and half-Irish and that adds up to large almond eyes, a little tilted nose, pink bee-stung lips, and warm ivory skin. Her hair is shiny jet black and she wears it short and kind of punky. She dresses kind of punky, too, but not too much, not to the point of really weird. And aside from being overwhelmingly gorgeous, there's something about her that sets her apart. A lot of ninth-grade girls operate in clusters, all giggles and whispers, a bunch of lumpy clones. Kim's got a mind like a steel trap and she doesn't try to hide it. Kim O'Hara is independent and cool, real cool. She can demolish you with a calm lift of her perfect eyebrows.

I don't really know her to talk to. I think she only goes out with older dudes.

I'm sitting two rows behind her. Miss Marino is conjugating an irregular verb and scratching away on the blackboard. I can't keep my eyes off the way Kim's hair comes to a tender point on the graceful line of her neck. Every time she moves a little, the gold safety pins dangling in her perfect earlobes catch the light. Without stopping to think, I make a paper airplane and shoot it over to her. It lands on her shoulder. She turns around and I smile. Kim gives me that killer look, one eyebrow raised, shrugs off the paper, and turns away. I feel like an immature jerk.

"In third-person plural, please, Mr. Szabo," Miss Marino says.

What? I don't know what she's talking about. I can't even think of a wise answer that would make Kim take notice. The Mouth strikes out.

George Miller rattles off the answer to Miss Marino's question and it's something easy—and now Kim O'Hara's gonna think I'm simple.

After lunch I see her opening her locker in the hall. I get over there fast and start twiddling with the lock next to hers.

"Hi," I say.

She nods noncommittally.

She's got her locker open and I see the poster pasted on the door. "I like Springsteen, too," I say. "Ever see him in concert?"

"Mmmhmm," she says. She's about to go away.

"Listen, I want to ask you something." Say something, mouth! "Uh—I'm thinking of getting my ear pierced and—uh—did it hurt?"

"Just for a minute," she says, "like a pinprick, that's all."

"Where'd you have it done?"

"There's a jewelry store on Sixth that'll do it free, but you've got to buy a pair of fourteen-karat studs," she says. She gives me a long look. "I could do it for you, with an ice cube."

I'm ecstatic. I feel like I'm getting somewhere after all this time! I mean, if she's going to draw my blood—and I wanted an earring anyway. I'd better check which side is the right one. I don't want to give out the wrong message, especially in my neighborhood. "Hey, great!" I say. "You're on, whenever you—"

I'm interrupted by a blow to my back that smashes me against the lockers. It's Bear, with a gap-toothed grin.

"I been looking for you," he says. "Today's the day."

"What for, knucklehead?" my mouth says. I think I just made the situation worse.

"You been chickening out the side entrance." He guffaws unpleasantly. "I'll be waiting for you, chicken."

Kim is listening to this and I'm destroyed. The

bell rings and she gathers her things and goes on down the hall.

"Today," Bear repeats ominously. He lumbers away, saying, "Cluck, cluck, cluck, cluck."

If he's waiting at the side entrance, I could go out the front. But he could fake me out and be at the front. Or maybe he's got lieutenants watching all exits. Maybe Jo-Jo and Garrity could set up a diversionary maneuver—hell, I don't even want to talk to them about it.

I cut my last class and leave school early. That takes care of one day.

4

SEEMS THAT I'VE GOT A TEMPORARY REPRIEVE. WREStling season has started and Bear is on the team, so he has to report to the gym right after school. I still have to keep an eye out for him around the neighborhood, but my exit from school is covered—at least for as long as wrestling lasts. I wish Bear great success on the team and hope they'll overlook his minor infractions, like eye gouging or rib stomping.

I'm delirious with new found freedom. I walk home with Garrity and I wind up hanging out at his place for a while, so I don't get home until the middle of the dinner hour. I find Cecilia's in an uproar.

"Where do you think you've been all afternoon?" Maggie says furiously. "Find that cat!"

"What?"

Maggie is vibrating with tension. "The word is the

24

health inspector is on the street, so hurry up and *find that cat!*" She's glaring at me.

"Okay, okay," I say. "You didn't have to wait for me. Anybody could've taken her upstairs, for crying out loud!"

"She won't pay attention to anyone else and besides, I can't leave my station!" Maggie explodes. Since Lorraine has turned up, Maggie won't leave the cash register for anything—which leaves Lorraine hovering over her with nothing to do.

This health inspector situation looks serious. Bob is frantically wiping down the bar, and Ellen, who likes to toss her golden mane, looks strange with it tied back in a rubber band.

The place is filled with customers and I don't want to make a scene. "Katie," I call softly, as I wander nonchalantly between tables. "Here, Katie!" I fail to understand why Katie should get us in trouble with the health inspector. A lot of laws make no sense at all. Katie's *immaculate,* cleaner than a lot of our customers, especially the artists. Maybe we should take a stand on this. Maybe Dad should make this a test case.

Dad passes by me on his way out of the kitchen. "Find that cat!" he mutters. He doesn't look happy.

Katie likes to nap under tables. That way, she enjoys the warmth and good smells and murmur of conversation and still has some privacy. She's very sociable. If she's picked Herb Lee's table, or another regular's, there's no problem; I can go under and get her. I ask Herb to take a look. No luck.

Then I see a striped tail protruding from beneath the tablecloth at five. There's a man I've never seen

before, sitting by himself. He looks awfully formal—
navy blue suit, striped tie, crisp shirt. I watch with
amazement as he turns the shrimp over and over
again on his plate. Then he's stirring the creole sauce
and seems to be looking for something in it. He picks
up his wineglass and sniffs at it for a long time before
he drinks. I wonder what he's doing. He *couldn't* be
a health inspector. . . . They don't *normally* sit down
and eat. . . . He seems totally absorbed and happy.
Katie's tail is gently waving over his highly polished
shoes.

I casually saunter past the table and whisper,
"Katie." She rubs against my leg.

The man at five notices me and looks up in a
contented daze. "Bon appétit," he says.

"Yes, sir," I say.

All I have to do is keep walking to the kitchen
and Katie will most probably follow—that is, if she
wants to.

I almost get to the swinging door when Katie
crouches low, her tail twitching, and catches the bottom of four's tablecloth. I can't believe she's doing
this; she *knows* how to act in a restaurant. Maybe she
thinks I called her to play. Maybe I woke her right out
of a mouse-hunting dream. Her front claws are in the
hem and she's pulling. The table is occupied by a couple who only have eyes for each other; the steaming
bowls of gumbo in front of them are untouched.

For a split second, time freezes, and with horror,
I see the scene in slow motion. Katie is pulling at the
tablecloth, it is moving, the couple are oblivious, and

the hot soup is starting to slide. No time to grab Katie.

I whip over and pick up a bowl in each hand just as the tablecloth goes, silverware clattering on the floor, the flower vase spilling.

"Hey, wait a minute!" the man says angrily.

"We're not finished!" the woman chimes in.

The bowls are burning my hands and I replace them at triple-speed, splashing on the bare table.

"What the hell—?" the man says, furious.

"A spot on your cloth, sir," I say solicitously, quick thinking all the way. "Have a fresh one out in a jiffy."

The lump under the wet zinnia-topped tablecloth on the floor must be Katie. I scoop up the whole thing any which way and rush for the kitchen.

I sigh with relief when I get through the swinging doors and unwrap Katie. She is upset; her tail has bushed to twice its size. Katie is very sensitive and not used to being treated this way.

"Get that cat upstairs," Cajun Jack mutters.

"Okay, I'm going, I'm going," I say. "I bet it's a false alarm anyway."

Ellen comes swinging through with a full tray. "Who is that guy at five?" she says.

I shrug. I scratch behind Katie's ears while she calms down.

"He is *weird*," Ellen says. She's unloading dirty dishes and picking up salad plates. "He wants a *bite*-size portion of goulash and that's the *tenth* bite-size thing he's ordered. And he keeps leering at me and saying 'bon appétit'! I don't have *time* for this!" Ellen loses her cool easily. I bet she's upset about having to tie her hair back.

"He can't be an inspector," I say. "He's too flakey."

"No sense in taking chances," Cajun Jack says. "The Board of Health, they cited Isle of Napoli last week. Get that cat *upstairs now.*"

I pick up some fried catfish and hush puppies for us and I'm on my way. Over my shoulder, I tell Ellen, "New cloth and silver for four!"

"What? What?" Ellen shrieks.

I disappear fast.

Usually I stay in the kitchen and eat and do homework and shoot the breeze with Cajun Jack until I go to bed. Katie and me, we're a lot alike. We like to be where the action is. Katie doesn't come upstairs until I do and then she curls against me in my bed for the night. So I'm not going to lock her up here and leave her lonely. I'll stay and keep her company.

Katie doesn't meow a lot. If I left her in the apartment by herself, she'd wait at the door in silent anxiety. Sometimes she looks at me and gives me that soundless meow and I can't refuse her anything.

I take the breading off Katie's part of the catfish —it's too peppery for her—and we eat together.

I like to watch her wash up. She licks her paw and goes over her face again and again before she's satisfied. A cat's saliva has a deodorizer in it, so when they wash, they're not just keeping clean. It's to make sure they can't be scented by an enemy. That's why they always cover their deposits, too. Cats' ears have a whole lot of extra muscles so they can turn them in lots of directions and hear all around. And they can see a moving object from enormous distances. Amazing animals, cats, absolutely perfect for hunting and survival, but not in city conditions, what with traffic and people like Bear Abbott around. Katie's smart; she won't ever go out the front door. Her territory is the restaurant and the apartment, and she rubs her face against chairs and table legs and me to mark her claim. She's my cat, all right, and I love her. After a certain point, though, watching her wash gets kind of boring and I don't feel like getting into my homework just yet. My room is the size of a postage stamp and there's nothing to do. I'm wondering if the health inspector panic has ended and I'd like to see what the guy at five is doing now.

I check the mirror before I go down. If I'm disheveled, Maggie's sure to say something; she gets very overbearing with me. I smooth my hair. It's too long right now, so it puffs up over my ears and looks dumb, but I'm going to get a haircut soon. I'll try the Astor Place barbershop where all the cool people go. I flex my arm. My bicep's growing. I don't look especially wimpy, in spite of the problem with Bear.

I think I'm getting to look more like Dad. A lot of people say so. My Grandma Van Dorn is convinced I'm the image of my mother, but I've seen photographs and there's no resemblance—first of all, she was very fair. I think Grandma wants to believe that so she'll have something left of Cecilia. She sure fought hard to get custody of me. I'm real glad it turned out that I live with Dad, but I feel bad for her. I definitely ought to visit this weekend.

Katie is occupied stalking a marble, so this is a good time to leave. I go downstairs.

The guy at table five is gone. Ellen looks hassled and I help her bus.

"You know what he did?" she says. "He ordered every single dessert on the menu and he took exactly one bite of each and left the rest! It's like cleaning up for a party of six!"

"Was he a good tipper at least?"

"Fair," she says. She never says "good," no matter what. I think she's waiting for a Howard Hughes type to come in.

"Does my dad know him?"

"He never saw him before in his life."

"Maybe he's an undercover scout for some other restaurant, stealing our recipes," I say. No, my imagination's running rampant; nobody knows or cares that much about Cecilia's. "I wonder why he—"

"You're always looking for reasons, Andy. Some people are just *strange*. Accept it." She shrugs and stacks a bunch of plates on my arm. "I used to work in a fast-food place and there was a guy that came in and ordered a hot dog every day. Every day, he'd throw away the frankfurter and eat the roll."

I bring the plates into the kitchen and scrape them. Cajun Jack is too busy to talk. I go out front again and I see Maggie at the door, putting on her coat and looking grim. I go over.

"Hey, Mag. How come you're leaving?"

She sniffs. "I seem not to be needed here."

I follow her glare toward Lorraine, behind the

cash register. There's a line of people waiting to pay and it looks like she's even slower than Maggie.

"Your dad said to give her a turn." She sniffs again. "If we're short at the end of the night, it won't be *my* fault."

"She's just temporary," I say.

"Doesn't look temporary to me," Maggie says ominously.

There's something about Lorraine that makes me nervous, too. She's not even Dad's type. Look, it's been twelve years since my mom died, so, yeah, he's dated, mostly very attractive airheads, but he's never brought anyone home or upset the whole restaurant for them. I can't figure out if he *sees* something in Lorraine or if he's just adopting a pound puppy. She looks a little better since he's been feeding her all the time; she's filled out some and her face isn't so pasty white anymore. But she looks a lot like a chipmunk, something about her jaw. I don't know what's going on here.

"Hey, Mag," I say. "Take off your coat and get back there before she messes everything up."

"I don't know," Maggie says doubtfully. "Your dad said—"

"You can do it, Maggie!" It's not like her to give up an inch of territory without a fight. She must be really worried. "Come on, Mag, show her who's boss."

She straightens up purposefully. "Right, I'd better take over before it's chaos."

I watch Maggie march over and then the Chipmunk backs off. The Chipmunk wanders away from

the register and sits by herself in the corner, looking
lost. Maggie looks up at me and winks. I wink back.
Over the years, Maggie has bossed me and milk-and-
cookied me and nagged me to death. This is the first
time in the history of Cecilia's that Maggie and I have
been allies.

5

It's late Sunday afternoon. I've been at Grandma Van Dorn's all weekend, since after school Friday. There's not much to do here, but I'd let a lot of weekends slip by without seeing her, so . . . Grandma's been working on her needlepoint and we've been watching a lot of TV. Not MTV, though—Grandma hates it. We watched a Van Halen video together once, and she said, "In my time, those people would have been declared insane and shunted out of sight." I knew enough not to bring my Beastie Boys tapes along this time.

We're having tea out of thin flowered china cups and I'm watching my manners and not slurping. Morgan—Grandma's chauffeur and handyman and you name it—brought in a silver tray of crustless tiny sandwiches. Grandma nibbles at them. I could gulp down five at a time, but I restrain myself and take small bites.

". . . and how are your grades now, Andrew?" she's saying. Her eyes are the color of faded violets. She must have been very beautiful once.

"The semester's not over yet, Grandma."

"But you must have some idea."

"Well, a sprinkling of B's, I guess." I don't add that the B's are sprinkled among a lot of C's. The kids that get the best grades are not necessarily the smartest; they're just the most willing to play the game.

"I hope you're trying." She sits very straight in her chair, fighting her arthritis. "If you wanted to go to medical school—or law school—someday, I'd be happy to cover the tuition."

"I know. . . . I don't like school that much," I say. "I mean, I like seeing my friends and everything, but—"

"You don't belong in public school, Andrew. Perhaps if you went to Philips Academy . . ."

"There's nothing wrong with my school, Grandma. I just get bored, doing homework and memorizing things I don't care about and—"

"Would you like some sugar cookies?"

"Thanks." I help myself.

"What does interest you, Andrew?"

"Oh, I guess rock and—uh—skateboards . . ." My big interest is girls, especially the inscrutable Kim O'Hara, but I don't tell Grandma that. "And I like to write. . . ."

"I meant your future plans."

"Oh. I don't have future plans," I say. Tenth grade

is about as far in the future as I can think right now. All I know is I want a life of adventure.

"Would you rather have cocoa or soda?"

"No thanks, tea's fine."

"I'd like to *do* something for you, Andrew." She says, sighing. "Cecilia and John did so well at Philips." John was her son. He died in Vietnam. His photograph, smiling in uniform, is on the big stone mantel next to my mother's. Cecilia was the baby of the family.

"You know, Cecilia was accepted at both Radcliffe and Mount Holyoke. If only—" Her mouth clamps down on the unsaid words, fine lines radiating from her lips.

I know what she's thinking. If only she hadn't gone to the Art Students' League and met my dad. "She was *happy*," I say. Cajun Jack told me they were crazy in love with each other. . . .

"I won't spoil your visit by talking against your father," Grandma says. Her skin looks like fragile old parchment. She looks out the window in the direction of the rose garden. "It's been such a cold winter. The Tropicanas will be all right; they're tough, just like me." She suddenly smiles and I wonder if my mother had a sweet smile like that. "It's the Blanche Moreau that worries me."

She gets up from her chair. Changing position is an effort and she tries not to let it show. I see her wince, though, as she straightens her legs. She crosses the room and stands at the window, framed by faded chintz curtains. "I don't know if Morgan hilled them properly. He's getting old."

I follow and stand next to her. I'm always surprised that she's really shorter than I am. She holds herself so straight and tall.

The wide lawn is brown now, with patches of snow here and there. The dark green gloom of pine trees dominates the background. Years ago, it was all big estates here. Now almost everything has been subdivided, but Grandma's big old house is still alone on the hill. There were Van Dorns in North Bay when Northern Boulevard was called the King's Road and this was a Tory outpost. There even used to be a street called Van Dorn Place. It was changed to Seaview Lane when the new development was built a couple of years ago.

"I'd like you to think about spending the summer here, Andrew."

"Grandma, I don't—"

"There'd be lots for you to do. At the club, I see young people around the pool and—"

"I'll come out for a weekend and—"

"You could have fresh air and the beach and . . . a better environment. . . . Well, the summer is still quite a way off, isn't it? . . . If you'll spend Christmas vacation here, we'd get a tree. We'd have a real old-fashioned Christmas."

"No, Grandma, I don't—"

"I want to give you all the advantages you're entitled to. You can see that, can't you, Andrew? You're old enough to *choose* where you want to live. It's not up to the courts anymore and—"

"I've told you, Grandma. . . ."

I'd never leave Dad, I *love* him and Cajun Jack,

I *like* living at Cecilia's. I like my life just the way it is. I've told her that so many times. And Katie wouldn't make it here either. I brought her with me once; she spent half the time hiding under a bed and the other half tearing up the Aubusson carpet.

One thing that crosses my mind is that here I wouldn't have Bear to worry about. But then, I wouldn't have much of anything else, either.

"Well, I always hope you'll bring some life into this old house. You're always welcome." Grandma looks at me and looks out the window again. "My poor Souvenir De La Malmaison. Those lovely old roses are a bit tender for this climate."

I slept in John's old room last night and it smelled of mothballs. Half the rooms have been closed off. A visit is okay, but I'll be glad to get home. My Adidas bag is on the Persian carpet, all packed up and ready to go.

"I'd like to come for Christmas, honest I would, but— If it could be *all* of us, you and me and Dad. He's a great guy, *everybody* likes him and— Why can't you—"

Grandma shakes her head.

"But *why* can't you—"

"He let Cecilia die," she says.

"He didn't! He did not! She had good doctors and everything! *She* was the one who didn't want to tell you she was sick. . . . She thought the chemo would work and you'd never have to know. . . ."

"Cecilia wouldn't have kept that voluntarily from her own mother! We used to be so close, before that wild man—Lazlo and I never got along, he was *never* right for her, but—" Grandma's voice is shaking and she pauses until she has it under control again. I feel sorry for her—she's standing rigid, hugging herself with her arms—and I'm mad at her, hating the things she's saying. "He kept her away and neglected her and put her in a slum and let her . . . I could afford the *best* of medical care. She should have been at New York Hospital, where all the Van Dorns . . ."

"It wasn't like that, Grandma!" Dad had told me all about it. There was a good chance for remission and Cecilia didn't think Grandma would ever have to know. Even when she lost all her beautiful hair, she wore a wig and managed to keep it from Grandma. It was for Grandma's sake, because she'd had so many losses already, John and . . . And then, when the chemo didn't work, it all happened so quickly. Dad gets tears in his eyes when he talks about her. Cajun Jack said Dad took good care of her, he did, and she had good doctors. Nothing more could have been done—it was just that Grandma never had time to get used to the idea, so she had to blame someone. Cajun Jack said my mother was a very gutsy lady.

"Where do you get your information, Andrew?" Grandma says quietly.

"Cajun Jack told me! He was there with them the whole time!"

"Oh, yes. The convict."

"I think I'd better go, Grandma," I say coldly. Cajun Jack used to live with us when I was little, to split the rent, before the restaurant got off the ground. Dad took me to the circus and the zoo and introduced me to fantastic foods, but it was Cajun Jack who made sure I brushed my teeth and had clean socks.

"Oh, Andrew." She smiles that sad, sweet smile. "I promised myself I wouldn't say a word this weekend, I really did, I so wanted you to have a pleasant time."

I can't help softening. "I know, Grandma. It was good to be here again. . . . I really have to go if I'm going to catch the 4:35."

"I don't like the idea of your taking trains and subways. . . . Are you sure you don't want Morgan to drive you?"

"The train's fine, Grandma." Morgan used to drive me here when I was younger. He's getting so old, driving with him is taking your life in your hands. Morgan has been with the Van Dorns for more than forty years; now they're all alone in this big house, and he still calls her "madam" and she still calls him "Morgan." I don't even know his first name. I wonder if they ever sit down and watch TV or eat together when nobody's around. Probably not.

"At least take a cab from Penn Station. . . ."

"I take subways all the time, Grandma."

"I wish you wouldn't. . . . All right, then. If you must go." Grandma moves to hug me. She's awkward about it; she doesn't hug easily, not like Dad, who'll hug anybody who comes into view. "Promise at least to think about Christmas."

She feels very thin in my arms and I inhale her fragrance, the same fragrance that was on the sheets and pillows and towels. When I was little, I called it "Grandma's smell." Now I know it's lavender.

6

I COME UP THE SUBWAY STAIRS AND ON THE CORNER OF Sixth Avenue, I see Bear. I'm pretty sure it's Bear; his back is toward me, but I recognize the lumbering bulk and the maroon jacket. He hasn't spotted me yet. There's no way I'm going to go past him.

I double back and walk all around the block the other way to avoid that corner. It's cold. My fingers feel frozen even in gloves and I stick my hands in my jacket pockets, letting my Adidas bag dangle from my arm. The wind is whipping my hair around. The cold wouldn't have mattered that much if I could have gone straight home, but this detour makes it twice as far and my cheeks are stinging.

Maybe it wasn't even Bear. I feel so stupid, going the long way around just in case. I think this is some-

40

thing I'll remember about myself all my life and it'll make me feel small every time it comes to mind. I'd rather be a hero, but it seems awfully dumb to face up to a beating if there's a way to avoid it. So if I'm doing the smart thing, why does it make me feel so rotten?

Cecilia's is quiet when I come in. Cajun Jack is talking to Bob at the bar while he wipes down. Ellen is setting up, with Katie following her and batting at the dangling ends of tablecloths.

I'm about to say, "Hey, I'm back!" when I notice Dad and the Chipmunk at one of the little tables. They're holding hands on the tabletop; they're in a bubble all by themselves.

Then Ellen chirps, "Hi, Andy," and Dad looks up like he's coming out of a dream. He comes over and I get the welcoming hug, but I have the feeling I interrupted something.

"I'm gonna take my stuff upstairs," I say.

For just a moment, the living room looks tiny after Grandma's big house and then I readjust and it's cozy again. Something is wrong, though. The couch pillows are all plumped up like no one's ever sat in them and my copies of *Rolling Stone* are stacked in a neat pile on the coffee table. I like to keep them spread out, so I can find the issue I want at a glance. And my schoolbooks are missing from the floor.

I go into my room and there are my books, piled up in the chair. I always do my homework on the living room floor and besides, I don't like my schoolwork near my bed, where I have to see it and be reminded of assignments I haven't done before I go to sleep. My bed! It's all made up, with the blanket pulled up stiff and no mark from my head on the pillow. It looks like a damn army barrack!

I hurl the Adidas bag into the corner and go storming downstairs.

"Who's been into my stuff?"

Dad looks up like it's hard to pull himself out of the Chipmunk's eyes. "What?"

"My stuff! It's all messed up!"

The Chipmunk speaks in a wispy little voice. "Oh, I'm sorry. I thought I—"

"Lorraine was good enough to straighten up for us and you should thank her, Andy."

"I had my magazines a certain way and now I can't find a damn thing!"

"I know what you mean. The trouble is we've been bachelors too long," Dad says with a smile. "It's time to clean up the mess."

"It's *my* mess and I want it left alone."

"I didn't mean to—I guess I should have asked first," the Chipmunk says, oozing hurt feelings.

"You sure as hell should have! What were you doing in my room anyway?"

"I told you to thank her," Dad says, mad.

"Jeeze, what's next? Curtains?"

"I was thinking of maybe blue . . . to match the . . ." the Chipmunk says.

"Oh, horse pucky," I mutter.

Dad is up and gripping my arm hard. "That's not the way you talk to a lady. An apology is in order." His voice is in his very low, barely in control, fuming mode.

"Sorry," I mumble. I go away for one weekend, *one* weekend, and the whole place is out of whack. The worst part is that Ellen is listening to this and seeing me being treated like a kid! I skulk upstairs.

It's late night and I've been dreaming the kind of dream I don't ever want to wake from. Kim O'Hara lifts her eyebrow in her most challenging way and slowly removes her scarlet T-shirt. Her head is on a centerfold's body and I slowly move closer. . . .

Something wakes me. I lie in bed and feel Katie against my leg. I have my hand on her fur and think I might have gotten its silky texture mixed up with Kim O'Hara's hair. I try to reenter the dream, but it's no use. It's gone.

Something woke me. I usually sleep through just about anything—cabs honking, the bar crowd downstairs, even police sirens. The one time I had trouble sleeping was in the summer at Grandma's. The crickets kept me up all night.

Everything is quiet but I sense something and I'm alert, listening. Then I hear Dad laughing softly. The walls are barely one step up from cardboard and I can hear his bed creak. I'm about to get up and go in his room to ask what's so funny when I hear another laugh—and this one is soprano. The Chipmunk. He's got the Chipmunk in his room!

I lie rigid in bed, barely breathing. He has never, ever brought one of his women into the house before. Everything's dead quiet again. If I strain, I think I can hear them whispering. I don't want to hear them.

I have this miserable feeling gnawing at me. I wish I was someplace else. I feel dumb, like a fifth wheel, and I don't even know what's getting to me. So Dad's got a woman in his room, so what? I know he's not a hermit. But what's a strange woman doing in *our house*? In my mother's bed, even!

I'm embarrassed and miserable. I don't even think the Chipmunk's that pretty, except for her eyes. Cecilia was a whole lot prettier. Why did this one have to get her little claws in him?

I try to go back to sleep and I can't.

Something is gnawing and gnawing. The whole idea of sex going on next door is getting to me—if that's what's going on and I'll lay odds it is. Fathers aren't supposed to act like bantam roosters, not where their own sons have to know about it!

I try to doze off, but I'm listening for the sound of the front door to tell me that she's leaving. I hope she's not still here when I wake up in the morning.

A couple of months back, Dad was kidding me about whether there were any cute girls in school and stuff like that. I made the mistake of mentioning that I want to go out with Kim O'Hara. All of a sudden, he turned serious on me.

"You're growing up so fast," he said. "I guess I've neglected talking to you about—"

"The birds and bees?" I said. "Don't worry, we get all that in school." I knew everything long before that, anyway.

"That's good," Dad said. He hesitated. "I want to be sure you're responsible."

"Responsible?"

"If you go out with someone—this Kim O'Hara, for instance—you owe it to her to be *responsible.*"

"Oh, right," I said. "I get you." I ended that conversation fast. Oh boy, he was talking about birth control! He thought I was up to that and I sure wish I was, but the sad truth is the chance hasn't come up.

I hate feeling that I'm nowhere near the man Dad is. I'd be ashamed for him to know how little experience I've had. I'd be more ashamed if he knew the way I ran from Bear Abbott this afternoon. He ought to have a macho son, and here I am, uptight and squirming because the Chipmunk is next door.

I don't like anything about this. She'd better not be moving in on us. I want everything to stay exactly the same—me and Dad and Katie and *no rodents*!

7

WE ALWAYS START DECORATING CECILIA'S FOR CHRIST-
mas a month in advance and then we keep everything
up until past New Year's because it looks so nice and
everyone likes it. It's that little space in the day before
dinner prep; no one else is in yet. Dad is up on a ladder
tacking gold tinsel high over the bar as the Chipmunk
feeds him more. She has to get into everything! We
have a Norwegian spruce at the front entrance and
I'm stringing the little white lights. Our apartment is
too small for a tree and we spend more time in the
restaurant anyway.

Dad comes down from the ladder. "That's it for
the tinsel. What do you think?"

It's in big swags against the dark wood and it
looks great.

He gets the box of red velvet bows and the three

46

of us start trying them on the pine branches. The Chipmunk is working near me. She looks a lot better than when she first came in. I guess it's all that good food Dad keeps plying her with. She's smiling and having fun, and Dad is, too. I'd be having more fun if she wasn't around.

"When I was a kid," she says, "we used to make popcorn and string it. . . ."

"In Hungary," Dad says, "they have candles on the tree. All those flames flickering . . . I don't like colored balls. The little lights come close, but it's not the same." He sounds wistful and the Chipmunk picks up on it immediately. She's always trying to please Dad.

"Do you want candles?" she says. "I'll run out and get candles. . . ."

"That's a fire hazard," I say. Anybody would know that.

"Here comes the star," Dad says. Every year, the tree has the red velvet bows and the big gold star on top. When I was very little, Dad or Cajun Jack would lift me and I'd put it on. They'd measure how tall I had grown over the year by how far I could reach. I guess Dad forgot all about that, because he boosts the Chipmunk up and lets *her* put it on top. It doesn't matter; I know I'm getting tall.

D.K. and Cajun Jack are in first and after a while, Maggie, Bob, and Ellen come drifting in. Everyone says how nice Cecilia's looks, except for D.K., who only knows a few choice phrases in English, but he grins and nods on his way to the kitchen. Cajun Jack sprays snow on the front window and it looks just about perfect. Dad's in a *very* good mood and he has Bob give everyone a glass of wine. Maggie is even talking to the Chipmunk tonight. There's the loud sound of Chinese rock from D.K.'s radio in the kitchen and for once, Bob doesn't even yell at him to turn it down. When Dad is feeling expansive, it's contagious, so Cecilia's is about the best place in the world to be tonight. Maybe Dad is so happy because decorating satisfies his artistic bent.

Most of the time, everyone eats together at the big table in back before we open up. I'm about to join them when Dad pulls me aside.

"We have to talk," he says, and leads me up to the front.

"What about?" I say.

We sit down on bar stools out of earshot.

"Lazlo, do you want salad?" the Chipmunk calls. Jeeze! He's perfectly able to get his own salad if he wants it!

"Okay, I'll be there in a minute." He pours himself a shot. "It gets so hectic around here. We never get a chance to talk alone."

"I know, Dad." That's because the Chipmunk is always hanging on to him.

"Well, this is what I want to tell you. . . . You know, Lorraine's living in a rattrap in the West Forties with a horrible roommate and it's ridiculous."

So was she going home to Des Moines?

"Ridiculous," he continues, "when she could be living here."

"Here?" I echo. "What do you mean here?"

"With us." He watches my face to see how I'm taking that. "You like Lorraine, don't you?"

"She's gonna live with *us*?" Tell me this isn't happening, Dad.

"She's a little shy. You'll love her when you get to know her better. She needs time to blossom."

"The apartment's awfully small, Dad. For three people." I wish she would do her blossoming someplace else.

"I know. So I want you to go out of your way to make her feel comfortable. Don't let her think she's crowding you, okay?"

"The apartment's awfully small," I say.

"We thought we'd wait to get married. This way, you can get to know each other better and—"

Married! Dad wants to marry the Chipmunk! "She's not that pretty," I say.

"She's not pretty," he says, beaming. "She's beautiful."

"You want to get *married*?" It's even worse than I thought.

"Lorraine's very special. You'll see, Andy. . . . It's time to have a woman in our lives again."

"Isn't that kind of—permanent?"

"I love her," he says simply.

I can't believe this. He's turning our lives upside down and he's got this goofy grin on his face.

"So aren't you going to congratulate your old man?"

What can I say? He's on top of the world. "Congratulations, Dad." I choke on it.

He puts his arm around my shoulders and gives me a hug, good feelings spilling out all over the place.

The rest of the night is a blur. It's Friday night, so I'm busing. Between stacking plates and resetting, I'm trying to get used to the idea. The Chipmunk is going to be my *stepmother*! The thought of that blows my mind. Just what I never needed!

"An extra setting for table three please," Ellen says.

Weekend nights are busier, but not bad; all the tables aren't filled all at once. Ellen and I work together easily, with time to kid around with the regulars—hardly any strangers in tonight. Herb Lee comes in early and then goes across the street to get ready for his show. Dad's at the front, meeting-greeting-and-seating. Maggie has successfully defended her territory from the Chipmunk, so Lorraine is just hanging out around Dad. Once in a while, she helps out with a beverage order; that's about all she knows how to do.

I bring a load of dishes on a tray into the kitchen. D.K. has his radio turned down to only semi-ear-splitting. He's chopping green peppers and beating time to the music simultaneously.

"How's it going, Andy?" Cajun Jack says, stirring the goulash.

"Okay."

"Busy out front?"

"Not bad." I wonder if Cajun Jack knows yet. I'm dying to talk to him, but he's grabbing orders from the carousel and putting out plates and stirring, so this is not the time. Maybe Cajun Jack can talk some sense into Dad later.

So the night goes by, normal under the circumstances. Fried catfish and hush puppies, a big call for jambalaya tonight, Ellen automatically reciting the special, "Chicken paprikasch Cecilia, boneless chicken breasts in sour cream, onion, mushroom, and dill sauce, heavily flavored with paprika." We're running low on shrimp Creole. D.K. is deveining some more in the kitchen. A newcomer asks about the palascinka and Ellen recites prettily, "Paper thin small rolled pancakes with apricot jam filling topped by caramelized sugar coating. I'd definitely recommend them." It's taken Ellen awhile to memorize the menu, but she's finally got it all together.

By midnight, most of the tables are empty, with a handful of people finishing up coffee. The bar is going strong, supplemented by comics from across the street, drifting in when their acts are over. Ellen gives me a cut of her tips and I'm about to go upstairs, when Herb Lee comes rushing in, waving a newspaper.

"Has anyone seen this?" he says to the room in general.

"What?"

"Tomorrow's paper! Hadley Addison's restaurant review! Listen to this, folks!"

We crowd around him as he reads.

"It is a rare pleasure indeed to report on a serendipitous new find. Cecilia's has a slow and easy ambiance and rather unprepossessing decor—"

"Unprepossessing? What does he mean, unprepossessing?" Dad says, flaring.

"Wait," Herb says. He continues, "—but the unlikely combination of cuisine of the Louisiana bayou and the Austro-Hungarian Empire works here and becomes more than the sum of its parts. The obvious freshness of all ingredients, the loving care in preparation, and the skillfully original reworking of what might have been Budapest and New Orleans clichés in lesser hands add up to an adventure in good eating."

"Clichés!" Dad explodes.

"Let me see that!" Maggie grabs the paper. "From liberally seasoned chicken paprikasch to the piquant hint of anise in peppery crayfish gumbo . . ."

"Someone, get Jack," Dad says. "Jack!"

Cajun Jack rushes from the kitchen, trailed by D.K.

". . . and the desserts are sublime finales, with smooth Dobos torte a perfect follow-up to the hot after-swallow glow of the Cajun specialities, and rich New Orleans crème brulée soothing the palate deliciously after the joy of spicy three-meat goulash. The basic concept of this small restaurant works—and works gloriously. The service is rather slow, though friendly, and—"

Ellen bites her lips at this.

"—and the staff is awkward, e.g., the sudden changing of tablecloths at inopportune times—"

I blush, while everyone else looks puzzled.

"—but minor quibbles notwithstanding, Cecilia's is a delightful discovery, one where honest and interesting cuisine can be enjoyed in convivial surroundings at surprisingly moderate prices. Here is a future star in the firmament of Manhattan's restaurant scene."

"Oh, wow!" Bob says.

Maggie looks up from the newspaper. "He gives us three stars!"

"Three stars!" Cajun Jack says. "From Hadley Addison!"

There is a stunned silence as the newspaper is passed from hand to hand. "Hey!" Ellen says. "It's the weird guy at table five, the other night! Hadley Addison. I thought that name was familiar when he signed his charge. . . ."

"Why didn't you say something?" Cajun Jack says.

"I didn't realize until just now."

Everyone groans.

The newspaper reaches Dad and he reads excerpts aloud again, savoring them. ". . . obvious freshness . . . adventure in good eating . . . joy of spicy three-meat goulash . . . You know what this means? Cecilia's is on the map!"

"We've made it. Oh, man, we've made it!" Cajun Jack says.

Everyone explodes now and the celebration starts. There are drinks on the house all around and everyone's laughing and hugging. Cajun Jack starts singing "Bon Temps Rouler," which means "let the good times roll," and they're sure rolling as everybody claps hands in time and Dad is snapping his fingers and doing his version of a soft shoe. Then Lorraine is dancing, too, whirling around and around with him. I'd forgotten she's a dancer. She's as graceful and light as a puff of dandelion on the wind.

Dad knocks on a glass to quiet everyone down

and get their attention. "As long as we're celebrating," he says, grinning from ear to ear, "I'd like to announce the engagement of Lorraine Anderson to Lazlo Szabo."

With all the excitement about the column, I'd almost been caught up in the good feelings . . . then— wham! Maybe someone will tell Dad he's making a big mistake. I'm counting on Cajun Jack.

"Way to go!" Cajun Jack shouts.

"All right!" The good times are rolling seriously and there are toasts being drunk and Bob is pouring liberally, splashing, and joy is rampant at Cecilia's.

The only ones who aren't one hundred percent into it are me and Katie, who comes out from under table two and stretches lazily.

8

It's the morning after the night before. The Chipmunk wasted no time in moving in. I need to go to the bathroom and she's in the shower. Then I hear her flushing the toilet and I die with embarrassment. When I finally get in, it's steamy and lacy panty hose are hanging from the rod. Her makeup is all over the sink; there's a million tubes and jars. When Dad sees it, maybe he'll realize it takes an awful lot to make her look not that great.

The three of us are bumping elbows all day. There's not enough room for her clothes and they're piled up on the living room couch. Dad's talking about taking a dresser out of my room, but where's my stuff supposed to go?

"Sorry. I guess it's kind of crowded," she says.

What was her first clue?

Dad even had to go down to the men's room in the restaurant to shave.

"We'll have to get a bigger place," he says.

There aren't any bigger places above the restaurant! I think he'll realize this will never work. He's in high spirits anyway, because of Hadley Addison's article.

"Andy, I want you busing tonight and Lorraine can give Ellen a hand. Maybe D.K. can come in early. . . . We should be getting more of a crowd. . . ."

There's a whole bunch of people out on the sidewalk before we even open up. Then, when the doors open, every table is filled right away and more are coming in and the bar is three deep. And this looks like an uptown crowd, too—furs, sequins, three-piece suits.

Dad is adding chairs to make tables of two into four and the aisles are getting narrow. "Keep things moving," he tells Ellen; "turn them over fast."

"Can you get our order here, miss?"

Ellen sprints to table three.

The calls are coming from all directions.

"Ah—we don't have a menu!"

"I'd like some water right away, and where is the wine list?"

"Pardon me, miss. We've been waiting a long time. . . ."

The Chipmunk is picking up menus and redistributing them. As she passes me, she whispers, "See that man at the bar, the one with white hair? That's the President's Advisor on Foreign Policy!"

Ellen brushes by me as she rushes to another table.

"Could you *please* take our order!"

"I'd like the three-meat goulash, but without green peppers, and can you make that *two* meat, veal and beef only, and not too much gravy. . . ."

"Miss, we've been waiting a long time here!"

"Three martinis, please, one with a twist, one olive, and one on the rocks, and a strawberry daiquiri, *if* you have fresh strawberries, and if not, make that a gin and tonic, no—uh—make that a vermouth cassis, better yet, two vermouth cassis instead of the one with an olive, and we'll order later. . . ."

I start clearing the first group of appetizers. There's no room for a tray stand or tray. I can manage six plates on my arm; that's about my limit.

A crowd is coming in the door. I see that model, what's-her-name, the sexy one who does the Mayhem perfume commercials. Dad is looking tense. He's steering more people to the bar to wait for tables.

"Ellen, keep it moving! Turn them over!" he mutters at her as she scurries past.

"I'm trying! I'm trying!"

"Try faster!"

Dad's going to have to hire more help, and soon.

Someone plucks at my sleeve. "Could you get a waitress over here, please. We *finished* the entree an hour ago!" The remains of goulash are coagulating on their plates.

Ellen, next to me, mutters, "Get this table cleared!"

"I'm trying!"

"Do it faster!" The strands of hair on her forehead are wet.

The Chipmunk dumps plates of pecan pie in front of a party of four. "What is this? We haven't ordered entrees yet!"

"Miss, a menu when you get a chance. . . ."

"Check, please!"

Hadley Addison's column just came out; maybe it'll calm down later. I hope we can make it through tonight.

Dad comes tearing through. "Speed it up! I've got people waiting for tables!"

"Miss, this isn't our soup!"

I charge into the kitchen. I can tell the passage of time by the stacked dirty plates, waiting to be scraped by D.K. They've gone from eight inches to three feet.

Ellen runs in behind me. "Where are my orders?"

Cajun Jack is sweating. The carousel is full. "I can't read your damn writing!"

She picks up an armful of plates. "Rush my orders!" she yells on her way out.

"Chop faster, dammit, D.K.!" Cajun Jack shouts. "I need more celery chopped!"

D.K. looks murderous. The tail of his snake is twitching frenetically. "She—it! Sohn oh beesh!"

I grab an armful of salads and hurry back into the pandemonium.

"This check is wrong. . . ."

"This isn't jambalaya! I ordered jambalaya, miss."

"Waitress! Waitress!"

Ellen starts to cry.

The people at the bar have been waiting there too long and are getting drunk. Bob looks catatonic and is chanting his mantra. The President's Advisor on Foreign Policy is completely sloshed and is indiscriminately fondling all the rear ends protruding from the bar stools. Dad has to leave the door to bounce him.

The Chipmunk spills creole sauce on a sable jacket.

I hear Ellen reciting the specials. "Chicken paprikasch Cecilia," she sobs. "Chicken breasts in a sauce of onion, dill, and apricot jam topped with caramelized sugar."

Everyone's yelling at me to clear faster. I try for eight plates on my arm and can't make it. They crash and the floor is strewn with hush puppies.

"Palascinka," Ellen continues bravely, "Little boneless rolled pancakes stuffed with . . . heavily stuffed with—paprika and—and paprika."

Someone around here has got to keep calm, I think. I stand off to the side for a minute and try taking deep breaths. This is a time for cool heads. I count from ten backward. I review my vocabulary. "Pandemonium, n. 1: the abode of all the demons; 2: the infernal regions; Hell 3: (not cap) a place like Pandemonium; a wildly lawless or riotous place; wild uproar; infernal noise or tumult." Oh, God!

There's a jam-up at the cash register. We only take Visa and all these people are waving American Express at Maggie. Maggie is checking their ID's and writing down addresses so she can send them bills. The line keeps growing. The people coming in get into shoving matches with the crowds trying to leave. Maggie is shouting above the din. "Visa only, read the sign! Visa only, read the sign!"

Can Cecilia's ambiance survive this? I don't know if even Dad can do anything to make these customers come again. His eyes look glazed; his famous charm is missing.

I hustle dishes back to the kitchen. There are now two stacks of dirty plates, four feet each.

We've run out of meat. D.K. is wielding a butcher's ax and eyeing Katie, who knows enough to take off.

Ellen comes through, tears rolling down her cheeks. "Table two just left. Hold their gumbo!"

"What? What?" Cajun Jack bellows.

D.K. is slinging orders ready for pickup onto the counter. Each time a plate is ready, he's supposed to ring his bell. Now they're mounting up faster than Ellen can get them and there's no room for more and D.K. is banging his bell nonstop and cursing, a paroxysm of bell ringing.

"Make him stop!" Ellen sobs.

A dignified elderly couple is at a table near the kitchen door. "What *is* that?" the lady says, irritated, as I pass by.

"Jingle bells," I say, flashing my brightest smile. "Christmas is coming!"

More dirty dishes to the kitchen. Three four-foot stacks and growing fast.

D.K. walks out.

Cajun Jack is frantically inventing meatless new

dishes—catfish goulash, catfish paprikasch, catfish crepes—and slogging them onto plates. In the rush and with D.K. gone, several of the catfish retain their heads.

"Take your damn orders!" Cajun Jack shouts at Ellen. "Hurry up!"

"Everyone's yelling at me!" Ellen wails. "Everyone's picking on me! Why *me?*" She gestures dramatically and knocks over the bucket of live crabs on the counter. They scramble for freedom through the swinging doors and scatter in all directions on the dining room floor.

It is Katie's finest hour. She hunts them down with exuberant leaps. One crab makes a dash for safety onto a rhinestone-strapped sandal. The owner of the sandal becomes hysterical.

Then Katie is in the center of the room, sitting on her haunches and noisily crunching as she separates meat from shell, crab juice dripping from her jaws.

The rest of the evening goes downhill.

When the place finally closes—even nightmares end sometime—everyone is drained. Dad looks pale and tense, more uptight than I've ever seen him.

At one point during this crazy night, Cajun Jack asked me to tell Dad we were running out of everything. I found him in a corner, arguing with the guy from the new laundry service. There was another one with him and they could have been twins—sharp dressers, flat faces, dead eyes—except that the other one had a broken nose. Their faces looked mad and their hands were chopping the air, and I was amazed that Dad had time for laundry problems in the midst of all the chaos. I went over, and Dad growled, "Go away, Andy! Find something to do!"

"But Cajun Jack said—"

"I told you to get away! This isn't your business!"

"But I'm supposed to—"

"Go! Now! I'm talking!"

Dad has never turned on me like that before. Now he's still tense and unhappy, but he's apologizing to Ellen for having yelled at her all night. He doesn't apologize to me; he doesn't say a word about it. First the Chipmunk, now this.

Ellen is collapsed in a chair, her face streaked with purple mascara. "The only one who was nice to me tonight," she says, "was D.K."

"*D.K.* was nice to you?" I say.

"Yes. Just before he walked out, he looked right in my eyes and said softly, 'Soo pid ah so.' I think that was Chinese for farewell." She looks exhausted. "It was nice of him to stop to say good-bye."

I have a feeling Ellen will be saying 'soo pid ah so' whenever she's in Chinatown. I don't have the heart to tell her D.K. was speaking English.

9

I'VE BEEN BUSING THE LAST FEW NIGHTS, UNTIL DAD hires a busboy, and between that and getting up for school in the mornings, I'm bleary-eyed.

They're still streaming into Cecilia's—though I've noticed no one's coming back a second time. Dad is meeting and greeting and projecting full Hungarian charm at everyone in sight, which is leaving his off-duty disposition a little frayed. He looks exhausted. The crowding in the apartment isn't helping, either. Me, Dad, and the Chipmunk are on top of each other, with no privacy and no room to turn around. The only time we get rid of her is when she goes to her dance class. I figure it's just a matter of time before Dad comes to his senses and the Chipmunk is out.

None of the regulars show up at Cecilia's anymore. Herb Lee says Hadley Addison's article ruined the place. The last time he was in, he didn't even finish his dinner and left to throw up early.

Maggie has taken to yelling belligerently, "Visa only! Read the sign!" at everyone who comes through the door. That's enough to make some people turn and go, and I guess that's a good thing, because Ellen and the Chipmunk can't handle the crush anyway. Ellen has gone from perky to borderline hysteria.

Dad hired a restaurant-school graduate to assist Cajun Jack. He started at 5:00 P.M. Tuesday night. At 8:30 P.M. Tuesday night, he walked out.

Guess who turned up with her parents? The beautiful Kim O'Hara! She smiled at me inscrutably. I guess I was rattled by trying to look cool with two armsful of dirty dishes—sort of "Andy Amid The Garbage"—so I tripped over my feet. It was my second crash of the week.

It's all a blur in my miasma of fatigue.

Tonight, Dad leaves the door for a minute and comes over to me. "Andy, you can quit and go to bed."

"But how—?"

"It's eleven o'clock; it should be slowing down," he says wearily, "and you've got school tomorrow."

"Okay, Dad." I'm more than ready to hit the bed.

"And, Andy?"

"Yes?"

"Thanks." He ruffles my hair and smiles. "Thanks a lot."

"Anytime." I sure hope he gets a new busboy soon.

I go upstairs. My body feels like lead. Normally, I lie in bed awhile and think about the day while Katie turns in circles until she finds the right spot, but this time I'm out as soon as I fall into bed.

It must have been a deep sleep. I don't remember dreaming anything. I'm not even sure what woke me, because Katie's not yowling loud or anything. She's just making this strange kind of hissing noise. I'm sitting up in bed. It must be late—no sounds from downstairs. It's pitch black, not even a crack of light under my door, so Dad and the Chipmunk must be asleep, too. Katie's eyes glow big in the dark.

I think I smell smoke and I feel confused because I'm still half-asleep. Katie is acting funny.

It's definitely smoke!

"Dad! Dad!" I've got Katie in my arms and she's clawing at my shoulder and I'm out of my room, yelling in front of Dad's door. "Dad! Fire!" The apartment looks okay; it must be the restaurant.

They stagger out, rumpled with sleep, the Chipmunk in a see-through lacy nightgown.

Dad smells it, too. "Go! Get out, quick!" he says to us. But Katie's jumped out of my arms and I'm trying to find her and the Chipmunk, the jerk, is looking for a bathrobe.

Dad is running downstairs. "Andy! Go outside. Lorraine, go!" he yells over his shoulder.

"Dad!" I hesitate and frantically look for Katie and then I run after him. I can feel my heart thumping. There's a fire escape at the living room window, but I'm not going to leave him down there alone!

The lights have been switched on downstairs and for a moment, I'm blinded. My eyes are burning. Dad has grabbed the fire extinguisher from the kitchen and he's spraying at the front, near the Christmas tree. There are billows of smoke.

"Dad? Is it okay?" I'm beginning to cough.

"It's out," Dad says. "I put it out." He opens the front door wide and lets the cold air in. "Just luck. Another minute and the whole place—"

The Chipmunk comes in, clutching a blue terry-cloth robe.

Dad looks mad. "I told both of you to get out! The whole place could have gone up!"

"But—" I say. It smells terrible. Acrid fumes are burning my nose.

"But nothing! You know enough to use the fire escape, right, Andy? What do I have to do, run fire drills? If this happens again, you get *outside*!"

"Okay, Dad, but—"

"It only takes *one* to use the fire extinguisher," he says, furious, "and I can get out fast if I don't have to worry about you. The fire escape, understood?" His voice is harsh.

"And that goes for you, too, Lazlo," the Chipmunk says. She's standing up to him; no one does that when Dad's this mad. "You call the fire department from outside! We *all* use the fire escape."

"Look, I had to try and save the—"

"I don't need a dead hero," she says, upset.

We're turning blue with the cold blowing in.

"You're right," he says. "I wanted to see . . . if I could. . . . You're right, Lorraine. Next time—"

"Next time!" I say. "What next time? What happened, anyway?"

"It's a good thing you woke up, Andy. Did you smell the smoke or hear something or—?"

"It was Katie," I say.

"So she's our heroine for the day," Dad says with a little smile.

I don't see Katie.

"What happened?" I say.

Dad shrugs. "It might have been the tree."

"The tree?" The tree wasn't lit and the scorched area isn't that close to it anyway. There's a whole section of the floor that's black and part of the carpeting at the front is burnt. How did a fire start in two places at once?

"A short or something," Dad says. "Listen, you're freezing. Go on back to bed. I'll clean up. . . ."

The air is still thick with smoke and the cold drafts from the door are whirling it around. Katie wouldn't be hanging around here. I go upstairs and find her, ears flattened back, under the bed. My clock reads 3:45. I'm shivering and I dive under the quilt. After awhile, I think I hear Dad and the Chipmunk coming up, and then I'm asleep again.

My alarm rings and I vaguely remember turning it off. The next time I wake up it's almost noon and sunshine is coming in the window. I've missed homeroom, social studies, science lab, and half of French.

I hear Dad and the Chipmunk whispering in the living room. There's been a hell of a lot of whispering since she moved in. I look around for something to put on and find a pair of jeans on the floor. I sleep in a T-shirt and Jockey shorts, I don't own a bathrobe because I never needed one before, and I hate having to get all dressed just to get out of my room. Granted, I was running around in shorts in front of the Chipmunk last night, but that was an emergency and I feel funny about it now.

I come into the living room.

"Good morning, Andy." The Chipmunk gives me a big smile, showing her overbite. She's always trying to be cheerful and friendly. I can't stand that.

"I overslept. I'm sorry, Dad," I say. He never lets me miss any school.

"That's okay. I didn't want to wake you," he says. He looks worn out. "Go get some coffee and sit down. I want to talk to you."

"Okay." The perc is hot and I pour myself a cup. I sit down on the chair across from them. I still feel foggy. "What happened downstairs? How bad was it?"

"The carpet has to be patched. There wasn't much damage—we caught it in time," he says. "I think we got rid of the smell. What do you think?"

I sniff the air. I'm still getting smoke. "I'll help clean up after school."

"You can skip this afternoon," he says. He rubs his eyes. "Andy, with all the hassle in the restaurant and the mess downstairs and—I want you to visit your Grandma Van Dorn."

"What? I was there last week."

"I'd like you to go this afternoon, just until things calm down around here. . . ."

"What things? You need me to bus, don't you?"

"I've got someone coming in tonight. You could use the break." He looks like he's trying to smile.

"What about school?" I'm mystified. He's never stopped me from seeing Grandma Van Dorn, but he's never especially encouraged me, either.

"Christmas vacation starts soon anyway, doesn't it? One week more or less won't matter," he says.

"A *week*? I don't want to go to Grandma's for a *week*. I was just there; I don't want to go now."

"I've already talked to her and—"

"You talked to her?" I don't believe this.

"—and made all the arrangements. Andy, I'd like you to go this afternoon, no questions asked."

"What's going on? How come you—?"

"Does everything have to be a big discussion?" Dad's face is a stone mask. "Make it easy, as a favor to me, no questions asked."

I choke down about a million questions. I don't get it. "How long am I supposed to stay?"

"Maybe through the new year, we'll see. She's an old lady; she'd like you there at Christmas. . . ."

My whole Christmas vacation? He was talking about more than a week; he was talking about—I glance at the Chipmunk and she smiles at me. Sure she's smiling—she'd won! All the crowding and whispering and covering up lacy nightgowns—I thought *she'd* be leaving soon! But I was the one in the way, I was the fifth wheel, the lovebirds were shipping *me* out! No, Dad could never do that. . . .

"Dad," I say, "do you really want me to go to Grandma's?"

I'm looking straight at him and he doesn't quite meet my eyes.

"Just for a while, Andy," he says.

I take a gulp of coffee and the hot liquid burns my throat and makes my eyes tear. I put the cup down and get up.

"Is it all right with everyone if I stick around long enough to take a shower?" I say, sarcasm and anger making my mouth taste sour. And, wouldn't you know, panty hose are dangling from the damn shower rod!

10

PENN STATION IS ABOUT AS DEPRESSING AS IT GETS. I'm going down the stairs to the Long Island Railroad from Seventh Avenue and I'm hit with the full pungent smell of urine and rancid hot dogs. There are two people at the bottom of the stairs, an old raggedy man with a homemade cardboard sign, the word "evicted" in large print, and a young woman with her hand out, chanting softly, "Any spare change? Any spare change?"

More homeless inside the station, bundles of rags, Hefty bags of possessions. I feel homeless myself —oh man, what a self-pitying spoiled-brat way to think when I'm heading for Grandma's damn mansion and these people don't have anyplace but a bench in the waiting room. I'm so damn lucky, right?

I made good time. I get my ticket and the train to

North Bay isn't in yet, so I go to the arcade and find Space Invaders. I play grimly, gritting my teeth, getting satisfaction from zapping everything on the screen. A lot of people I'd like to zap: Bear, the Chipmunk, the obnoxious lady who gave me a hard time at Cecilia's last night. And Dad, too. Especially Dad.

The train is announced on track nineteen and I go through the motions, swinging my Adidas bag, finding a window seat, taking my ticket out of my jeans pocket. One-way ticket. There are some newspapers scattered around, left by the morning's commuters, but I don't feel like reading anything.

I look out the window as the scenery races past. The way I am, I wise off and try to twist anything that happens onto the funny side. I don't mean hilarious, I mean just enough to make me feel better. That's the secret of Andy "The Mouth" Szabo. Like the problem with Bear; I find dozens of ways of describing him as a Neanderthal and that helps. If liking Kim makes me feel inadequate, I think of her as the Inscrutable O'Hara. Turning Lorraine into the Chipmunk made me lighten up about that whole thing. Even the chaos at Cecilia's—well, seeing the crazy side makes it bearable. I'd always rather laugh than cry.

Only now I'm staring out the window and there's no way I can make up a funny name for Dad or use a sarcastic adjective to make it all right. All my defenses are down this time and the bottom has just dropped out. Here's a guy that I trusted, *trusted* for almost fourteen years, and look what happens.

This train is a local and it's stopping at all the little towns. Elmhurst, Auburndale, some mystery towns announced in conductorese. North Bay is the end of the line. No matter what, this train is going to slowly but surely deposit me in North Bay, where Morgan will be waiting at the station. Too late to turn around now.

Okay, I try to understand Dad. I know he fought for custody of me, I guess in that first heat of mourning when Cecilia died. Maybe I shouldn't blame him that much for regretting it. Here's this good-looking single guy with a kid around all the time, getting in the way. I guess he really fell for Lorraine—why *her*?— and having me around is a major pain. Hormones or no hormones, I'm his *son*, dammit!

I've been at Grandma's for two days; it only feels like two years. Time sure flies when you're having fun.

I can tell Grandma's happy to have me here and she's gone out of her way to make me feel welcome, like a bowl of fruit and fresh flowers in my room and nice things like that. I appreciate it, a lot. *Someone* still wants me.

I don't have anything to do. I almost miss school, that's how bad it is. I've been taking walks around town after school hours to see where all the kids hang out. There was a bunch of jocks congregating at the pizza place down the block from the junior high. It was a big, noisy crowd, a lot of high-pitched squeals from the girls. I walked into the place and had a slice. Not knowing anyone felt strange. No one even noticed me or said a word.

I saw another group around my age, dirt-bag

types, down behind the deli. They were drinking beer
and smoking pot. We got to talking; I was asking what
kids do in North Bay and they thought I'd have to be
pretty tough, coming from New York City. Seems like
the city gets a bad rap in the sticks. Anyway, they were
friendly; if I were into getting wasted, I could be in the
group in a minute. I guess so much of their lives are
wrapped around being stoned that it's enough in com-
mon to cement a friendship. Too bad; one of the girls
was really pretty.

I saw some guys playing a pickup game of soccer
at the high school field. I stood around, watching,
but I couldn't find a way of getting into it. It looked
like fun.

I told Grandma about seeing some of the North
Bay kids, not going into details, and she said, "Oh, but
Andrew, those are the *townies*! You should be meeting
the Philips Academy group."

I don't know who she thinks I am. I've been in
public school all my life. I guess Dad would qualify as
a townie. I guess I'm a townie at heart, too. Anyway,
I don't think Philips Academy kids hang out; they get
bussed in from all over.

"If it were summertime," Grandma said, "you'd
be going to the pool at the club. I hope you're not too
bored. . . ."

"No, Grandma. I'm fine."

She'd like me to live with her for good. The way
things are going, it might even come to that.

I'm sitting in my room—John's old room—with a
notebook and pencil on my lap, looking out the win-

dow. I've got lots of time on my hands and a whole bunch of feelings choking me. I think of maybe trying a poem and I think sad, bad, had, mad . . . I am sad, I feel bad, I've been had, no room for glad, I am mad! It stinks. Well, set it to a rock beat and maybe it would work. I guess I really do like to write, considering. As far back as I can remember in grade school, writing was for discipline—"Write one hundred times, 'I will not throw spitballs.' " Orange Garrity is one hell of an artist; I wonder if he'd still like painting so much if some dumb teacher had made him *draw* something one hundred times for a punishment.

I miss Katie. It didn't make sense to get her all upset if it was only for a little while. She doesn't do too well in carrying cases, trains, or cars. Cats are very territorial and like familiar surroundings. Katie even hates it if I move the furniture in my room. I miss her, though. I know Dad and Cajun Jack are feeding her, but I wonder if anyone's playing with her. And she has no one to sleep with; I doubt she'd be welcome between the lovebirds. Maybe I'll have Morgan drive me down to pick her up. If this goes on much longer.

I am sad, I am mad. I am mad, I am damn mad! Dad's been calling here just about every night and I don't like how homesick it makes me to hear his voice. He keeps asking how I'm doing and I say everything's great. Look, if this doesn't bother him, it's not going to bother me, right? I go on about how nice it is at Grandma's, how big the house is, what a pretty town. . . . All the conversations sound pretty much the same.

"Hi, Andy. I wanted to call while I have a minute, before the rush starts. . . ."

"How's it been?" I ask.

"Busy."

"Maybe I ought to come home now. I could—"

"We hired a new girl to work with Ellen. Monica. She's training tonight, and I have a friend of Bob's at the door. So that'll help."

All kinds of new people at Cecilia's who I don't even know! "How's the new busboy?"

"He seems okay, a little slow still. . . . Andy, I want to know how you're doing."

"Oh, fine. No problem." I'm not going to *beg* to come home.

"Well, *what* are you doing?"

"Oh . . . I met some kids. You know, North Bay kids, and . . ."

"So it's all right?"

"Fine, Dad. It's great. A great bunch of kids and—"

I hear background noise of voices and dishes clattering.

"Wait a minute, Ellen, I'll be right there. . . . I've got to run, Andy. Just wanted to say hello. I'll call tomorrow when I get a break. . . ."

"Dad?"

"Yes?"

"I want to pick up Katie. I'll have Morgan drive me down and—"

"Hold on a minute, okay?" I can hear him say something about a party of six and then I hear Maggie's voice. This is a test. If he says there's no sense in upsetting Katie because he wants me home *soon,* if he tells me that . . . then I'm booking straight back to Cecilia's. Double time.

"Sorry, Andy. What were you saying?"

"I want to pick up Katie and bring her here."

"Okay."

Just like that. One word. I feel my stomach cramping. He wants me staying here, out of his way!

"Okay. So long, Dad." I don't even want to talk to him anymore.

Dinner is very early at Grandma's. Tonight, Grandma and I are at the big table in the dining room. Last night, it was trays in front of the television because I especially wanted to see a teen horror flick on cable, *Werewolf of Hollywood High;* it was a howl. Cajun Jack would have loved it. I could tell Grandma was trying hard not to look disgusted, and eating off a tray is not her thing. So I didn't tell her I wanted to see *Extra-Terrestial Surfers* tonight. She's trying extra hard to please me and I wish I was happier, for her sake.

The food here is different than I'm used to. I'd never thought of food in terms of colors before, but it's true. Cecilia's food is mostly reddish, paprika and red peppers and tomatoes and shrimp. I miss it. Here everything is basically white, a lot of white bread and mashed potatoes and milk.

Morgan serves rice pudding for dessert. I kind of stir it around with my spoon.

"If there's anything you'd rather have, Andrew—"

I can't stand being called "Andrew." She'll probably be calling me Andrew for the rest of my life.

"No, Grandma. This is good."

"—or if you have any special favorites—"

"It's fine. I like everything."

The hard thing about being away from home is the strain of being so polite all the time.

11

When Dad calls again on Saturday morning, I don't exactly rush to the phone. There's nothing left to talk about.

I take it in the study. The phone is on a big dark wood desk, with crooked carved legs. It must be an antique.

"Hi, Andy. How's it going?" His regular opening. What does he expect me to say?

"Fine."

"What've you been doing?"

"Things."

Long pause.

There's a silver-framed photo on the desk, of Cecilia and John. It looks like they're teenagers. They're laughing and they each have an arm around a big dog. Irish setter, I think. I would have liked to have known Cecilia.

"What kind of things, Andy?"

I shrug. "I want to pick up Katie," I say after a while, "and the rest of my stuff. I'll have Morgan drive me down sometime this weekend."

Another pause. "Andy, this is very hard for me to tell you. . . . Katie isn't here."

"What? What do you mean? Where is she?" He wouldn't have given Katie away, not Katie, not even if the Chipmunk asked him to. He *loves* Katie! But he was supposed to love me, too. My voice gets shrill. "What do you mean, Katie isn't there?"

"Andy, there was another fire last night. . . ."

"Another fire?" I sound like a damn echo. What's this with the fires? Maybe the Chipmunk is some kind of firebug. That's what happens when you take in just anybody that happens to fall into your restaurant. "What happened to Katie?" I'm afraid to hear.

"There was a lot of smoke and commotion, and the fire engines' sirens were wailing and—there were streams of water from the hoses and—"

"What happened to Katie?"

"We think Katie panicked and ran out in the confusion. She was missing this morning and—"

"No!" Katie!

"Andy, she's only been gone one night. We think she'll come back and—"

"She would have come home by breakfast if she knew how! She's lost. You know she's lost."

"I feel as bad as you do."

"No you don't."

"We looked all over for her this morning and we called her. . . . She's probably hiding somewhere. She'll find her way back."

She must be terrified. She doesn't go outside; she doesn't know anything about outside. "I'll come right home," I say.

"No, Andy, wait—"

"I have to find her!"

"There's nothing you can do. We've been—"

"I won't stay. I just want to look for her."

"Not now, Andy. Listen, I'll call you the minute we hear anything, okay? Today's just not a good day for you to come home. We'll keep calling her—she's a smart cat, she'll turn up. . . . Hey, I know how bad you feel, but—"

"Okay, sure, fine. So long." I hang up. Nothing, nothing is going to keep me from looking for Katie! He doesn't have to worry, I won't get in his way. As soon as I find Katie, I'm gone.

Grandma tries to talk me out of going back.

"I have to," I tell her.

"If you want a new kitten, Andrew, I'd be glad to—"

I almost hate her for that. "I don't want a kitten! I have to find Katie!"

"Well, if you must," she says dubiously. "Morgan can drive you down tomorrow."

"Grandma, I'm taking the next train out. And I'll stay over, just until I find her." They'll have to put up with me, that's all. I mean, they're not going to put me out on the street. That's probably against the law, anyway.

"Well, when do you want Morgan to pick you up?"

"I'll call. Maybe he can pick both of us up." Maybe.

Two dismal rides on the Long Island Railroad in four days—and they've been the highlights of this week. The train crawls along the tracks. I can't think of anything but Katie.

It's a cold, gray kind of day. At least it's not raining or snowing. Please don't let it rain before I find her.

It's thirty-two degrees. I hope it doesn't get any colder. She's an indoor cat. She didn't grow a winter coat.

Great Neck . . . Little Neck . . . Bayside . . . Douglaston . . .

She doesn't know anything about traffic. She must be so scared and bewildered.

She must have run from the fire engines and smoke and just kept on running until she was lost. Even one block away would be unfamiliar.

Auburndale . . . Woodside . . . Penn Station.

She was out all night! Where did she sleep? She's so choosy about her special places—my bed or the corner of the bar.

I rush through to the subway and the A express comes right away.

She trusts everybody. I think of the way she rolls on her back and allows her stomach to be scratched, legs limp in the air, eyes half-closed. She doesn't know about people being mean to cats. . . .

Fourteenth Street and the subway roars on. Next stop and I'm home.

Maybe if *I* call her . . . She knows my voice better than anyone's. . . .

I run from the subway exit. Sixth Avenue is full of shoppers, Saturday tourists, kids walking and looking around. The sidewalk is crowded with vendors hawking jewelry and leather goods. I run all the way, past the glassed-in sidewalk cafes on Seventh Avenue South, past the piano bars on Grove Street. Panting, I turn into Bedford, three blocks from Cecilia's. This is as good a place as any to start looking. She could be right around here, anywhere around here.

I call "Katie! Here, Katie!" with a lot of emphasis on the second syllable, the way I do when I call her for mealtime. She always comes running, skids to a stop at my feet. "Katie!"

I go slow, looking. She could be under any parked car, in any alley. I concentrate on every shadow. "Katie!" I stop and stand still after each call, so in case she hears me, she'll have time to come.

There are lots of people passing by and I feel like they're staring at me. I feel self-conscious, all by myself and calling "Katie!" as loud as I can. Okay, so it's not cool. I must look weird—but Katie needs me.

"Katie! Here, Katie!"

I turn into Commerce Street, past the Cherry Lane Theater and the Blue Mill Tavern. I look into a little patch of yard separating town houses. It would be a good, quiet place for her to hide—but she's not there.

When I get to Cecilia's, I rush to the door. I almost expect her to be sitting in front, waiting. . . . No. The spot is terribly empty. I look in. I can't see any fire damage from here.

I go around the block the other way. "Katie!" Past the pizzeria. "Katie!" Past the pottery store. "Katie!"

A girl and a guy with an NYU jacket are watching me curiously.

"I'm looking for my cat," I say. "She's lost."

"Oh," the girl says. "That's too bad."

"Have you seen her? She's a tabby, mostly gray and black stripes, kind of beige on her chest. . . ."

"No. Did you just now lose her?"

"She's been missing since last night." As I say the words, I realize how hopeless it is. She could be blocks from here. She could have gone in any direction. I don't know where to look.

"If you see her," I say, "she belongs at Cecilia's. Just down the street."

The girl looks sympathetic. "Sure. If I see a cat like that, I'll let you know."

"Thanks," I say. There must be a million tabbies in the city. No one's going to know that it's Katie. I wish she had a collar and address tag. It never seemed important before; she never went outside.

I go on halfheartedly. "Katie! Here, Katie!"

And then I think—maybe she came home by herself, maybe she's inside and sleeping right now! I should have checked at Cecilia's first.

I double back. The restaurant is closed, still too early for dinner setup. I go up to the apartment door and start to take my key out. I have a real funny feeling. Am I supposed to use my key or do I have to knock first?

12

CAJUN JACK ANSWERS MY KNOCK. HE LOOKS RUMPLED, as if he's been sleeping. I'm surprised to find him in the apartment and I'm relieved that it's him I'm facing, not Dad or the Chipmunk.

"Andy!" His big hand gives my shoulder a squeeze. "Hey, buddy!"

"Hi," I say and return his hug. "Did Katie come back?"

"No. I'm sorry." He rubs his eyes. "Don't worry, she'll turn up. Cats can find their way."

Maybe in Louisiana, I think, not in New York City. Katie doesn't have a chance—I've got to keep looking. . . .

"How're you doing?"

"Okay," I say. "Did I wake you or something?"

"I had to get up anyway. The kitchen's still one mess."

"Is that where the fire was? The kitchen?"

He nods. "We got most of it cleaned up last night, but—"

"Are we opening up anyway?"

"Sure we are. It's Saturday night! The fire won't stop us." He looks grim.

"How come you're here?"

"I stayed over last night," he says. "We were up all night and—"

Cajun Jack lives only six blocks away. Why did he sleep here? I thought Dad and the Chipmunk were looking for privacy. What is this, a ménage à trois?

"Does your dad know you're home?"

"No. What do I have to do, make a reservation?" I'm glad it comes out sounding bitter.

Cajun Jack starts to say something and then I can see him changing his mind. "He'll be back pretty soon; he'll be happy to see you, but—"

Sure he will. I'm about to say something about how I feel; I think Cajun Jack will be on my side. I'm interrupted by the sound of a key in the door.

It's the Chipmunk. I stiffen.

"Andy!" she says. She looks surprised.

"Hello," I mumble.

She gives Cajun Jack a defiant look. "I'm back."

"Lazlo, he won't like—" he starts.

"I'm not going. This is where I belong," she says, her little chipmunk jaw jutting out. She's carrying a little suitcase.

I don't know what's going on. Were they breaking up or something? Too much wishful thinking.

"He wants you out," Cajun Jack says. "If there's trouble tonight . . ."

"What's happening?" I ask. "More chaos at Cecilia's?" They ignore me.

"Maybe I can help," she says.

"He doesn't want—" Cajun Jack says.

"You could use an extra pair of eyes, couldn't you?"

"Lazlo won't go along with that."

"I'm back," she says stubbornly, "and that's it!"

"Well, talk to Lazlo. I have to get downstairs. Andy, I'll catch you later. You staying for dinner?"

"I guess. I'll be looking for Katie."

"Then I'll put aside some Hoppin' John jambalaya and crème brulée." He grins at me. Those are my very favorite things. "And stop off in the kitchen before you go back to North Bay."

"I'm not going back *tonight*," I say. "Not until I find Katie."

Cajun Jack looks from me to her. Everyone is acting really weird. "See you later then," he says.

The door closes behind him.

The Chipmunk and I look at each other and look away. The silence between us is awkward.

She breaks it first. "I'm sorry about your cat."

"Thanks a lot," I say, dripping sarcasm.

"She might be in heat or something. She might be out, you know, catting around."

"That is the dumbest thing I've ever heard!" I explode. "Katie is spayed! There's so many unwanted kittens already; I wouldn't bring any more into the world. That is so stupid! Do you know how many kittens are abandoned or put to death or—"

"Hey, hold it!" she says. "All I said was, I'm sorry about your cat, okay?"

"Well, I'm going to stick around until I find her. *If* it's all right with you. *If* you don't mind. If my presence won't cramp your style."

That seems to get to her. "Look, I've had a really rotten day and I don't need any more hassles. Do whatever you want to." She gets a cup of coffee and puts it on the table. She's going back and forth from the kitchen with milk and sugar. There's a lot of extra, restless motion. She kicks the suitcase out of her way.

I go into my room. It looks pretty much the way I left it, except the bed has been made. I open my drawers and check my stuff. Everything is still there. I go back into the living room.

She's drinking her coffee in silence, ignoring me. The air is bristling with nervousness. Maybe she and Dad really did break up.

"What's with the suitcase?" I ask. I hope she's not moving more of her things in. "Where've you been?"

The Chipmunk is twitching. "I was supposed to stay with a friend, but I changed my mind," she mutters at me in a tone that tells me to mind my own business.

"What happened?" I ask.

"About what?" She looks defensive.

"You said you had a rotten day. Before."

"Oh, that. For openers, I went to an audition this morning and I didn't get it and I *know* I'm a better dancer than—well, I . . . I didn't get it. For the chorus of the new Sondheim musical and I *wanted* it, damn it! And now—I'm waiting here to fight with your dad and he's the most stubborn—so I'm not up for any more snotty comments from you, okay?"

"Snotty? *Me?*" I say innocently.

"You've got it. Snotty."

A gracious winner she's not. "What are you complaining about?" I say. "You got what you wanted."

"What I wanted?"

"You're here and I've been shipped out to North Bay."

She looks surprised. "North Bay? What's that got to do with me?"

"Oh, nothing," I say, dripping acid. "Not a thing."

"Lazlo said you were having such a great time there. . . ."

"Yeah. Yippee."

"Well, talk to your father about it." She looks mad. "It had nothing to do with *me*. And I didn't stop any cats from getting spayed, either!"

She pulls up her suitcase and marches into the bedroom. I hear drawers rattling and closet doors opening and slamming. Then there's a long silence.

I have to go look for Katie some more. I'm about to leave when the Chipmunk slowly comes out of the bedroom.

"Andy?" she says softly.

"What?"

"Did you think your father sent you away because of me? Because of my moving in? Is that what you've been thinking?"

Hearing it said straight out like that embarrasses me. I look at the floor.

"Oh, you poor kid . . ."

That about does it. Who's a poor kid! The mouth opens but she continues before I find suitable words.

"You're all wrong, you know. . . . God, I wish he had told you! . . . You sure jumped to some wild conclusions. Oh, Andy." She shakes her head sadly. Then she takes a step closer to me and looks at me meaningfully. "Did you ever hear of the Galucci brothers?"

"Yeah, I've heard of them."

"Consider it," she says.

Consider the Galucci brothers? What do mob connections have to do with anything? Boy, she is one flakey chick. I'm mulling it over when the door opens and Dad bursts into the room.

"Andy! What are you doing here?" He doesn't look happy to see me.

I don't know if she's been telling me the truth. "I think I live here," I say, checking his reaction.

"He's been thinking a lot of things," the Chipmunk puts in.

Dad whirls toward her. "I want you gone tonight!"

"Lazlo, I'm in for better or worse."

"It'll be worse and I want you out. And you"—to me—"you're supposed to be at your grandmother's." He sounds furious.

"That's some welcome for your son," the Chipmunk says. "No wonder. He thinks you don't want him anymore."

"What?" Dad says.

"Because of me. Because of us getting together," the Chipmunk says.

I'm embarrassed again. "That's okay, Dad. I mean, if I'm in the way . . . North Bay is okay and . . ."

"What? . . . Not *want* you? Are you kidding?"

I shrug.

"What's going on here? You're my *son!*" He kind of half laughs incredulously. "You think I don't want my own *son?*" He's looking at me like I've lost my mind.

His son. If he ever saw me wimping away from Bear, he wouldn't be so quick to claim me.

"You sent me away, didn't you?" I say.

"Hey, wait a minute. What's wrong with visiting your grandma?"

He's not giving me a straight answer. Something is wrong. "I didn't volunteer to go, Dad."

"Temporarily," he says. "It was temporary. Don't you know you're everything I've got?"

I glance over at the Chipmunk. She's standing with her hands on her hips. "The two of you sure have trouble talking to each other! Why don't you *tell* him, Lazlo?"

"Tell me what?"

"How much I love you," Dad says quickly. The expression on his face is pained. "What kind of father do you think I am? How could you think for a minute I'd give you up? That's some vote of confidence. You've got to trust me a little!"

"I'm sorry, Dad."

"No, Andy, don't be. I should have explained

somehow. . . ." The expression on his face is such a combination of hurt and love and worry that it's hard to look at it.

"Love is never having to say you're sorry," the Chipmunk says profoundly.

We both turn to her. "Now what does that mean?"

She hesitates, wide-eyed. "I don't know."

Dad moves in for a bear hug and I feel his hands pressing hard against my back. His voice is muffled, his lips are next to my hair. "I'd never let you go, no matter what." He holds me for a long moment and I feel like a little kid, comforted by the warmth of his body. "I guess I thought you'd know, without having to be told. I love you, Andy, and don't you ever doubt it. I *love* you."

"Me, too, Dad." I feel funny with the Chipmunk standing right there and listening to all of this. I fight to keep my voice steady. It feels good to have Dad's arms around me. It feels good to be home again. If I knew where Katie was, everything would be okay.

Dad breaks the hug and holds me at arm's length. His eyes seem to be getting watery, or maybe it's just the way the light is hitting them. He takes a deep breath. "I want you to go back to your grandmother's tonight."

"But, Dad—"

"Not for very long, Andy."

"But *why?*"

"I thought you were having a good time. The house and the kids and—"

"It's okay for a couple of days. I want to be home now."

His hand gently caresses my cheek and runs up to ruffle my hair. "Just for a while," he says softly. "Please. I have to know that you're safe."

Safe? I see lines on his face that I've never noticed before. I feel prickles running up my back. The Galucci brothers! "Dad—are you in trouble with the mob?" I whisper.

13

Finally Dad is cornered into telling me the truth.

"Every business on the street goes along with the Galucci brothers. It's the price of being left in peace." He looks tired. He passes his hand over his forehead before he continues. "Until now, it was mostly small potatoes."

"*We* haven't gone along . . . have we?" I can't get rid of that funny chilled feeling.

He hesitates before he speaks. "We switched to the new laundry service, at twice the price. . . . The tablecloths haven't looked right since—"

"Those guys were the Galuccis?" They were right here at Cecilia's and Dad was arguing with them! I feel half-fascinated and half-scared.

Dad nods. "And garbage removal for all the stores in the neighborhood . . . A little here, a little there."

"Why didn't someone tell the police or—?"

"It's too subtle, Andy. There were no outright threats, just 'suggestions.' And it wasn't worth taking the chance. You go along and do the best you can, and it was a little skim off the top."

"It still isn't worth taking the chance," the Chipmunk says. "Couldn't we all go away or—?"

"No!" I see the muscle working on the side of Dad's cheek. "This is where I draw the line."

"But—"

"No!"

The anger on his face makes me afraid he's going to do something crazy. "What happened, Dad?" Whatever it is, it's bad.

"Hadley Addison's column. All of a sudden, Cecilia's is big-time. Crowds coming in. It attracted attention."

"What do they want?"

"Fifty percent."

"Fifty percent?" I repeat dumbly.

"A partnership. Half of Cecilia's! I said no."

"You said no to them?" I can't keep my voice sounding normal. "The fires? . . ."

"They could have torched us with gasoline. Those were just two little warnings to make me fall in line. 'Three strikes and you're out.' They want the right answer from me tonight."

"Dad, call the cops!" Everything I've ever heard about mob killings, bodies dumped in the river, cars exploding, is racing through my mind.

He shakes his head wearily. "Proposing a business partnership isn't against the law. I can't prove anything."

"But what are you going to do?" I say. My words spill out in a jumble. "Maybe fifty percent won't matter that much, I mean, if business is that good and people keep coming and—"

"You could open a restaurant somewhere else," the Chipmunk puts in. "Out of the city or— We should all leave and—"

"No! This is my place, mine and Cajun Jack's." The blood is rushing to his face. "That's Cecilia's name over the door and her paintings on the walls! And that slime is not going to own it!" His eyes are blazing.

I know how hotheaded Dad can get. I recognize all the signs.

"Lazlo, be reasonable," the Chipmunk says.

He turns on her furiously. "No! Cajun Jack and I put too much into it. I love this damn place and I'm not running. This is where it stops."

"Lazlo, please—"

"Don't start again, Lorraine. I defend what's mine." He takes a breath. "I told you to stay away. I want both of you gone."

"But, Dad—" I'm scared, proud of him for being brave, but mostly scared.

"It's all right," he says grimly. "Don't worry, Jack and I are ready for them."

Ready? He means they're armed, that's what he means! I don't know if Dad has ever used a gun. And Cajun Jack—he's an ex-con and he'll get in serious trouble! If—if they even come out of this. "Dad!" I

want to clutch his leg and stop him, the way I did
when I was a little kid.

"I won't go," the Chipmunk says. "If you can't be
reasonable, then let me help."

I can tell he's way past reason. His emotions are
going to carry him right into facing the mob! "I'm
staying, too," I say, my voice shaking. Everyone I love
is at stake.

"You can help by being out of the way."

"I'll stay out of the way," the Chipmunk says. "I
could be a lookout, I could warn you when—"

"No," he says. "Jack's taking the back door and
I'm taking the front. I don't want you in the middle
of it."

"How about the roof?" the Chipmunk says. "I'll be
perfectly safe on the roof, and I can see if—"

"Me too," I say. I can't leave when he's facing this.

"We're not playing kids' games," he says. "Andy,
go to your grandmother's tonight."

Go to your grandmother's with the old ladies and
children! Rambo, I'm not. I can't even stand up to
Bear Abbott. But this is my father and I love him and
if anything happens to him . . .

"Dad," I plead. "I'm a man. I want to help you."
I clamp down my lips before I start blubbering. "Don't
send me away now. Please, Dad."

"Let him be a man," the Chipmunk says quietly.

The wind on the roof is fierce. The Chipmunk is wearing a big down coat and she's huddled in a blanket that

she's got wrapped over it. I'm wearing all kinds of stuff under my ski jacket and I've got a wool navy watch cap pulled way down over my forehead. There's a flashlight and a quilt folded up at my feet. We're drinking hot coffee from the thermos that she brought up a little while ago. I feel the warmth of the cup through my gloves.

We're sharing a corner. She's looking out over one end and I'm looking over the other. There's no way we can cover the whole block, but I can see a good part of the street and she's watching the alley.

Dad didn't think anything would happen until after closing. The Chipmunk and I came up when the last trickle of people left Cecilia's. There weren't many people tonight, anyway, and no repeaters; I guess the word of mouth hasn't been too good.

I had to go downstairs to pee three times during the hour we've been up here. I don't want the Chipmunk to notice how nervous I am, but I guess she did. When she had to go downstairs, she kind of laughed and said, "Me, too."

We're not in danger, I don't think. If we see something, all we have to do is tell Cajun Jack on this walkie-talkie, from two birthdays ago, that I dug out of my closet. It's old, but it works. We promised Dad that if there was trouble, we'd go across to the next roof and get away and call the police. It took an hour to convince him to let us do this and then we had to swear on everyone's head that we'd take off fast, no matter what.

It's pitch dark up here. All I can see of the Chipmunk is her outline leaning over the edge. I see a match flicker and then the glow of the lit end of a cigarette.

"I didn't know you smoked."

"I don't. Not often, anyway. Only when I—" Her voice trails off.

There's a quarter moon and a handful of stars. Five flights down, the streetlamp on the corner throws a circle of light. All the lights in Cecilia's are out. I see a couple leaving the comedy club across the street. The girl's giggle drifts up to us. Everything looks slightly out of kilter from this view.

A car passes. Then the street is quiet again. I can't help looking for the outline of a cat.

"Bad things come in threes," I say. "The fires and Katie and . . ."

"And what?"

I can't finish the sentence. I can't think of anything happening to Dad. I've got to get my mind on something else, quick.

—or to Cajun Jack.

She picks up on my silence. I hear her catch her breath and then say harshly, "That's nothing but superstition."

"Sorry," I mumble. "That was stupid."

She loves him, too, I think.

I hear her sigh, a long exhale of smoke.

"I'm superstitious sometimes," she says. "My lucky potato is in my pocket."

"Your what?"

"My lucky potato."

"That's what I thought you said." I glance at her.

There's just a silhouette. I turn back quick, to scan the street.

"There's this guy. I used to see him all the time, on Forty-third and Eighth, you know, when I'd pass by, going to auditions and—anyway, he was selling lucky potatoes, dipped in his grandmother's well water, he said. Two dollars each."

"What was he, some kind of nut?"

"No, an entrepreneur. I guess you're too young to remember pet rocks? If someone can make a killing on pet rocks, why not lucky potatoes?"

"And you bought one?" I say incredulously. Another car passes on the street.

"Oh, not right away. I thought it was silly. But I kept seeing him there and everything was going sour for me. I've been dancing since I was five years old and I'm *good*, you know, and when I came to New York, I got into a show, but it closed after a couple of months and then—nothing. I kept going to all these auditions and—I was a replacement in the *Sugar Babies* chorus but that closed and then—nothing. A dancer doesn't have many years and I'm twenty-six and I started feeling really desperate. I was running out of unemployment, I couldn't even pay for class anymore, and so one day, I broke down and bought a lucky potato. I needed some magic and it couldn't hurt, right?" She sighs again. "I'm sorry, I'm babbling. I guess I'm nervous. Do you see anything?"

"No." Both sides of the street are empty.

"Nothing here, either."

"Well, what happened? Did you get lucky?" She's a flake, I think.

"At first, I thought, boy, I sure didn't have the two dollars to spare, and I thought I'd better just fry and eat the thing and go right back home to Des Moines and forget it. But that was the day that I fell into Cecilia's!"

"So your luck changed?" I ask.

"Lazlo is the best thing that ever happened to me!"

I feel embarrassed by the open, cornball joy in her voice.

"I'm not very worried about him," she says. "He always knows how to handle things. He's really so strong and—"

"I know," I say. "I'm not too worried, either."

We're whistling Dixie in the dark and we both know it.

It must be two o'clock in the morning. There's sand under my eyelids. I feel strangely hollow. My teeth are chattering and I don't know if it's only from the cold.

"How about more coffee?" she asks.

"Okay."

"Shine the flashlight here so I can see to pour."

"No, wait. The light— They could see us!"

"Just for a minute," she says. "There's no one here."

I check all along the street again. I turn the light on and turn it off quick. I feel my heart pounding.

The hot liquid spreads its warmth in my chest.

"I'm scared, too, Andy."

"I didn't say I was scared!"

"All right," Lorraine says.

"I am, though," I add.

I hear her soft chuckle. "There's nothing wrong with being afraid, you know. We'd be fools if we weren't. Basic survival instinct and all that."

We go back to quiet watching. There's no sound from downstairs. My toes are getting numb. I take the quilt and wrap it around my shoulders.

"I'm freezing," I say. "How're you doing, Lorraine?"

"Not too bad," she answers.

It's hard to keep my concentration on the street for all this time. But I keep looking. I won't let Dad and Cajun Jack down.

My lips are chapped; I guess I've been biting them. Lorraine and I have stopped talking, but the silence between us is not uncomfortable.

A few cars pass. I hear an ambulance siren from way up the avenue. It's a long time till morning.

Nothing happens. I start to yawn and then I remember with a shudder why we're here.

"Three o'clock in the morning is the dark night of the soul," I say.

"What?" Lorraine says.

"A famous writer's line; I forget which one. It's something like that."

"Dark night of the soul," she repeats. "That's good."

"I don't think I could write anything like that. I wish I could. Sometimes I want to be a writer and then I think why should anyone want to read what *I've* got to say. Do you know what I mean? It seems kind of arrogant." The hour of the morning and my fatigue and my nervousness are making me babble, too. We can't even see each other's faces. It's like talking to yourself.

"If that's what you want, go for it," Lorraine says. "A dancer assumes she's worth an audience. It's kind of showing off, I guess. It's not something to think about. You just *do* it, because you want to or need to or for whatever reason."

The moon is a pale sliver now. All the windows across the street are dark, except one. I wonder why somebody else has been up all night. There's steam rising from a manhole cover.

"I'd like to write screenplays," I say. "The way the street looks now—wouldn't that make a great setting? All I need is a plot and a typewriter."

"You seemed so—I don't know. I never knew you were into things like that," Lorraine says.

We've never talked before, I think.

It's getting lighter. I glance over and I can clearly see the back of her head, moving from side to side and up and down.

"What are you doing?"

"Relieving the tension in my neck. Try it, it helps."

She's as uptight as I am. I'm about to tilt my head to my shoulder when I see the car.

"Lorraine," I whisper. "Look!"

There's a car that's obviously slowing down in front of Cecilia's. It's creeping along and almost comes to a stop. My hands are shaking and I fumble with the walkie-talkie. I'm about to hit the button to call Cajun Jack when it picks up speed and drives away. We watch it disappear around the corner.

"Should we tell Cajun Jack?" I say.

"If it comes back." Lorraine is next to me. "It could have been someone looking for an address."

The car doesn't return.

Nothing happens.

I wrap the quilt around tighter. Outlines on other rooftops become crystal sharp in the clear air.

The sun rises and we watch in silence. Streaks of red mixed with gray cirrus clouds. I'm used to seeing the sunrise on picture postcards of mountains and lakes. I've forgotten that it happens in city skies, too. It is awesome.

The garbage truck comes down the street, clanking tin lids. Some early-risers are out and some late-risers are staggering their way home. The light goes on in the bakery. There's an old lady picking through a wastebasket. A dog-walker trots down the street, pulled by eight dogs of various sizes. I watch with amazement as the leashes somehow don't tangle. A large truck works its way past the parked cars. The sunlight is thin and cold.

I wonder how Katie spent the night.

The walkie-talkie buzzes. It's Cajun Jack.

"Come on down and get some sleep. I guess tonight wasn't the night."

"Okay." I'm glad to pack it in.

I don't see how we can stand guard forever. The hopelessness of Dad's situation washes over me. The Galuccis could strike anytime, any day or night.

14

I COULD HAVE SLEPT FOR A WEEK.

When I come out of my room, I find Cajun Jack dozing on the couch and Lorraine in the corner, doing pliés and stretches on the portable bar she's set up. She tells me Dad is downstairs in Cecilia's kitchen; I can smell the day's goulash cooking. We're all going about our business and listening for the other shoe to drop. I sit down at the table with some paper and concentrate on composing a notice. I print the words in big letters.

LOST CAT   LOST CAT   LOST CAT

Female tabby, gray and black stripes, beige chest, yellow eyes, small, one and a half years old, answers to Katie, very friendly, missing from Cecilia's Restaurant since Friday night, December 18. Please call if you've seen her.

106

I print it over and leave out "very friendly." She could be too scared to be friendly now. I make the letters bigger this time and I add "REWARD FOR RETURN." I'll worry about coming up with a reward later. It's worth anything to get my Katie back. On the bottom, I make columns of the address and phone number for people to tear off. I read it again. There are no special distinguishing characteristics; how will anyone know it's *Katie*? What else can I say? I think of the way she loves paper bag games and sardines and the sweet expression on her face when she's content.

I pass Maggie at the cash register on my way out. It's time for the lunch shift. I show her the sign.

"I'm going over to the library to have it Xeroxed," I tell her. "Got any Scotch tape?"

She reaches into the drawer and hands me the tape. She kind of shakes her head, as if I'm doing something stupid.

"It's only a cat," she says.

I can't even answer that. I slam out the door. Only a cat! Cats are the most graceful creatures on earth. Who but a cat can turn its body midway in air and land on its feet, or pack so much dead-aim energy into a pounce, or recline so elegantly? Maybe cats make people like Maggie nervous because they're not subservient.

On the way to the library, my focus is on hiding places, alleys, and doorways and under parked cars. I make one hundred copies of the notice; when those get used up, I'll make more. Somehow I've got to find her.

Only a cat! Who decided that *man* was made in

God's image? Maybe it's the other way around. Maybe God's in the form of a great orange tomcat with luxuriant whiskers.

I cover all the stores in a circle around Cecilia's. The dry cleaner says he'll put up my notice, but when I start to tape it on the window, he takes it from me and says he'll put it up himself, later. I have a feeling he'll throw it out as soon as I'm gone. The lady at the bakery clucks sympathetically; she tells me that strays look for food around dumpsters late at night. The pizzeria lets me tape it on the front door. The drugstore says no; if he lets everyone put up signs, his whole window will be cluttered. I put it on the bulletin board at the supermarket and I plaster every bus shelter and phone booth that I pass. Chique Boutique says they'll keep it in the corner of their window for a week. A lot of the people around here know me and most of them are nice. I finish up at Cecilia's and tape a sign on the door and at the front window. I hope black and white show up enough; I wish I could Xerox in bright red.

Dinner has started; there's not one familiar face, no regulars, and only a handful of uptown types. I go upstairs. Lorraine is in the living room, watching TV and chewing her nails. I sit around, waiting for the phone to ring. It doesn't.

Dad has put new smoke alarms all over the place. Suddenly, they all go off and Lorraine and I jump. False alarm. It was Cajun Jack making blackened bluefish.

Minutes tick by. We bring dinner up from downstairs and we both pick at it. I don't even know what's on my plate.

"You should try to catnap," Lorraine says. "If we're standing watch tonight . . ."

"You too," I say.

"I can't."

"Me either."

I'm not looking forward to being out in the cold. It's already dark. The uncovered window looks black and chilling. I see my reflection as I move toward it. The view from here is too limited. It'll have to be the roof again.

There's nothing for us to do until Cecilia's closes. Lorraine paces for a while and then she goes back to doing stretches. I stare at the phone.

I get up and put on my jacket. "I can't stick around here," I tell Lorraine. "I'll be back before closing."

"Where are you going?"

"To look for Katie." I remember what the bakery lady said. Stray cats would hide from the bustle of the day and come out at night.

"I'll go with you, all right?" She's as restless as I am.

"Okay."

She pulls on her big down coat.

If I'm going to have a prayer, I'll have to think like a cat. "I'm trying the quiet streets."

We're half out the door when she stops. "Wait. I'll take my umbrella."

"What, is it supposed to rain or something?"

"That's not why," she says.

We leave the bright lights on Cecilia's block and head west. Hudson Street is dark and deserted. We walk slowly past shuttered warehouses.

"Katie! Here, Katie!"

I'm glad Lorraine came along. I feel less embarrassed about calling "Katie!" when there's someone with me doing the same thing. Anyway, there's no one on the street to notice.

"Katie!"

I see a shadow move in a doorway. It's a cat! In the dark, I just make out stripes and a flash of something white.

"Katie! Katie!"

The cat moves away warily as I come closer.

"I think it's got white paws," Lorraine says.

I'm not sure. I go after the cat and she takes off in terror. "Katie!" She's somewhere in the alley. I can't see her. I stand and search among bits of litter and broken glass.

Lorraine catches up to me. "If it was Katie, she'd come to you."

"I don't know. Maybe she's so panicked that she'd run from anything." It hurts to think of all the things that could have happened to make her so frightened. It hurts to think of her living among garbage and glass shards. "Katie!"

"That wasn't her. I'm sure I saw white paws," Lorraine says.

It was too quick a glimpse in the dark to know for sure. "But she had stripes! I saw stripes!"

"Andy, thousands of cats have stripes."

We stay and call for a while and then I give up. It probably wasn't her, but I wish I could have had a better look.

We continue along the street. It's a clear, icy night.

"Katie! Here, Katie!"

I see something move under a parked car. It's a fluttering sheet of newspaper.

"At least it hasn't rained or snowed since she's been gone. That's something," I say. I glance at Lorraine. "What's with the umbrella anyway?"

"Oh, that. Well, you said you wanted to go along the quiet streets and I thought, just in case we ran into trouble—"

"The Village is mostly okay," I tell her. "And what good would an umbrella do?"

"When I lived in the West Forties, off Ninth Avenue—well, you know all the sleaze there. I'd have to walk home late at night after a performance and I had to work out a self-defense system. So I started walking along, swinging an umbrella, I mean in big circles all around me, and if someone looked scary, I'd start yelling every foul word I've ever heard of. And you know something? A lot of people steered clear of me."

"What kind of foul words?"

"Oh, things I would never repeat! We don't talk like that in the Midwest." I suspect she's blushing in the dark.

"So you're swinging the umbrella, saying this stuff—"

"Not *saying*, yelling and screaming. I had to out-crazy the crazies. See, violent insanity is so very unpredictable. Even the muggers and rapists tend to keep away."

My dad's going to marry the mad umbrella lady of West Forty-fourth!

"Well, it worked," she says defensively. "No one ever bothered me."

I start laughing. Even with Katie and the Galuccis on my mind, I can't help laughing. "I'm in the presence of an original mind," I say.

Lorraine looks at me, quick, to see if that's a putdown, and then she starts laughing, too.

Lorraine's all right.

When we get back to Cecilia's, dinner time isn't half over, but the place is dead. Dad is sitting at the bar talking to Bob, and Ellen is standing around looking into space. I'm about to go upstairs to get ready for the night's vigil when the phone rings. I leap at it—maybe someone's seen Katie!

"Hello?" I say hopefully.

The man's voice at the other end sounds hoarse. "Lazlo?"

"No, this is his son. Just a min—"

"Listen, kid." There's an ugly edge to the huskiness. "Give your old man a message."

15

I LOOK TOWARD DAD AT THE END OF THE BAR.

"Tell him, forget it," the hoarse voice continues. "Half of nothin' is nothin'." There is a short laugh that doesn't sound humorous. "But the boys don't appreciate his attitude. So tell him laundry charges are going up."

"My Dad's right here," I say. "I'll—"

Click.

The silent receiver looks malevolent.

I repeat the message to Dad. I think I remember it word for word. Dad calls Cajun Jack out of the kitchen and I repeat it again.

"Half of nothin' is nothin'?" Cajun Jack says thoughtfully.

"Does that mean we're off the hook, Dad?"

"I suppose. God, I hope so!" Some of the tension

has left his face, but he seems pained as he looks around the mostly empty restaurant. "Half of nothing . . ." A handful of tables are finishing dessert and a party of four is at the cash register and that's it. Normally dinner would be in full swing and Herb Lee and that crowd would be hanging out at the bar between shows.

"Hey, Lazlo," Cajun Jack says, "it's Sunday night before Christmas. That's always slow."

Dad looks dubious. "How much are we throwing out tonight?"

"Well—so we overbought. . . . We ought to close up Sundays, that's always slow and—" Cajun Jack is improvising. "Everyone's spending and buying presents, so they're not eating out, they got to save somewhere, right? It's got to pick up after the holidays. . . ."

"We're just hitting our stride, finally ready for a crowd and—" Dad sighs deeply. "At least the Galuccis are off our back. I can't believe it's really over! That calls for a drink." He smiles for the first time in days and gestures for Bob to serve himself, too.

I feel limp with relief.

"Man, I tell you, I didn't need that," Cajun Jack says wholeheartedly. "Trouble, stay behind me!"

"You think that's the end of it?" Dad can't shake all that anxiety in a minute.

"That's what they said, isn't it? That's the way I read it." Cajun Jack claps his hand on Dad's shoulder and Dad nods.

"Well, here's to sleeping at night and not looking over our shoulders!" He takes a drink and wipes the ring his glass has left on the bar. I can tell he's not ready to celebrate yet.

"Amen," Cajun Jack says.

We were amateurs at standing up to the mob. I don't even like to think about what could have happened. I just want everything back to normal.

"What makes the Galuccis think business won't pick up?" Dad says slowly. "Why would they lose interest in us so fast?"

Cajun Jack shrugs. "They don't know restaurants. . . ."

"No, it's too easy, Jack."

The party at table five gets up to leave and Dad goes over to give them some last-minute charm. I watch him and it's like he's doing an imitation of his natural ebullient personality.

"Come in again," he calls after them as they go out the door. That's not like him. That's almost as bad as "Have a nice day."

He comes back to the bar and takes another sip of his drink. "What do the Galuccis know that we don't?" he says.

The door opens and Herb Lee comes bursting in. Even though it's cold out, his face is shiny with sweat.

"The usual?" Bob says.

"No. A glass of milk. My ulcer's acting up." He pulls out a handkerchief and wipes his forehead. "It's a cemetery across the street."

"Empty?"

"No, big holiday crowd, but I had an audience of tombstones tonight. Not one laugh. They musta shipped them in from Forest Lawn."

I can tell Dad is busy thinking, hardly listening to Herb Lee. I feel sorry for Herb. He probably went into his desperate demented-chicken routine again.

"Hey, what's happening here?" Herb looks around. There's a line of milk on his upper lip. "Last time I was in, the place was a madhouse."

"A hotbed of pandemonium," I say.

"We've got it under control now," Dad says.

"That's good. I hate to see a good place ruined. It was crazy that night—gave me indigestion." That reminds him to take another swallow of milk. "Hell, I'm on again tonight. . . . What's the use, maybe I ought to quit show business. My ex-brother-in-law can get me a job selling aluminum siding. . . ." I've never seen Herb so glum. He's not even pretending to be up.

"We've worked out all the glitches," Dad says. "You can start having dinner here again."

"That night was crazy," Herb says. "I left just after you bounced the President's Advisor on Foreign Policy."

"You missed the best part," I say. "You missed the catfish goulash."

Ellen has joined us. "And Katie chasing crabs."

Mention of Katie gives me a stab. I'd do anything to have her back.

"D.K. walked out," Cajun Jack puts in. "We haven't seen him since."

"And Ellen was pushing boneless pancakes," Dad remembers.

"Maggie set a new high in belligerence," Bob says. " 'Visa only, read the sign!' "

That was the single worst night in Cecilia's history and tonight is probably near rock bottom in Herb Lee's record of misery, and here we are, egged on by Herb, reminiscing about the disaster and laughing our heads off. I'm almost light-headed with relief.

Dad seems to be somewhat apart, worrying a napkin. I'll bet he's still thinking about the Galuccis.

Herb is laughing the hardest, a manic look in his eyes; I sure hope he doesn't decide to throw himself off a bridge tonight. He raises his glass of milk. "Well, here's to Hadley Addison, folks!"

Dad looks up. "Has anyone seen today's paper?" he asks slowly.

Everyone's negative. I guess Cecilia's crew isn't big on current events. Well, Dad usually is, but he's had a lot on his mind.

"Do me a favor, Bob. Run down to the newsstand. . . ."

When Bob gets back, he hands the newspaper to Dad and everyone watches as Dad nervously riffles through it. Then he finds what he's been looking for and we see dismay spreading on his face.

"What is it?" Cajun Jack asks.

Dad passes it to him. "Guess what? The Galuccis read newspapers, too," he says harshly.

"What? What does it say?" I ask.

Cajun Jack reads aloud. "New York Dining by Hadley Addison . . . Sometimes it is a restaurant critic's unfortunate duty to retract a prematurely enthusiastic review. In this column, I recently awarded three stars to Cecilia's, a small Cajun/Hungarian bistro in Greenwich Village." Cajun Jack clears his throat. "Regrettably, the inability of the management and the kitchen to handle even a slight increase in diners forces my immediate reevaluation. The obvious lack of professionalism, an abundance of ill-conceived new dishes and disastrously lacking service earn, at best, a No Star rating. This is New York and no, Virginia, your Aunt Tilly from Budapest cannot compete in the Big Apple with a few old family recipes. My scouts tell me—"

Suddenly Dad punches the bar with so much force that I think he might have broken his hand. He gets up quickly, leaving the bar stool rotating, and stalks to the far wall of the room, his back to us.

No one says anything. Cajun Jack doesn't continue. He crumples the paper in his big hand and studies the floor. The gloom spreads. The twinkling lights and bright red velvet bows on our tree and the swag of tinsel over the bar are suddenly shabby and incongruous.

"Gotta get back for the next show," Herb Lee mumbles. "See you, folks."

Cajun Jack's expression is grim. "That first column made the Galuccis think we had a gold mine here and now this tells them Cecilia's is dead! Well, this is one *good* spot with *honest* food, no matter what some idiot scribbles." His eyes are flaring. He's looking at Dad facing the wall at the end of the room. "Lazlo," he calls, "we might be down, but dammit, we're not out!"

I wish Lorraine would come from upstairs. She'd know how to talk to Dad. I go over to him and speak to his back; I'd just as soon not see his face right now.

"The regulars—they'll come back. They don't care about Hadley Addison and his column," I say.

Nothing from Dad.

"And, Dad—we don't have to worry about the mob getting after us and. . . ."

"I never skimped on an ingredient." Dad's voice is ragged. "I looked for the freshest, the best. . . . This whole place was a labor of love, do you understand, Andy? It was all slow and careful cooking, never cornstarch. . . . I gave it my best. I loved feeding people and seeing them enjoy. . . ." He turns to me and I see his eyes are wet.

"Cecilia's will get back to normal," I say. "It was good the way it used to be."

"We'll be starting over. . . . We've lost too many regulars and . . . One damn column and everything we've worked for is mud!" He passes his hand over his eyes. "The overhead is going to kill us."

"Like the laundry charges?" I remember the voice saying they'd be going up.

"Like the laundry charges." The anger on his face makes me afraid; I hope he won't try refusing the Galuccis again.

"Are you going to pay them, Dad?" I ask.

He meets my eyes and the hurt pride on his face makes me look away. "Yes," he mutters. He feels ashamed in front of me! He wants to look good in my eyes, just as badly as I want to look good in his! I want to tell him I don't care; he doesn't have to be a superhero for me.

"I know, you've got to," I say.

"Life isn't all black and white, Andy. There are lots of gray areas." He doesn't have to justify himself to me, but I don't know how to tell him that. "I

wouldn't, couldn't give them half of Cecilia's. They'd
have to kill me first. But laundry . . . Sometimes,
you've got to compromise, Andy. At least for a while.
I hate it, but . . ."

"I know, Dad. It's okay." I feel like I could almost
tell him about Bear Abbott. I won't, but I could.

"You've got to know where you draw the line.
There are things you've got to stand up for, no matter
what. And otherwise, you do the best you can. Com-
promises!" He spits out the word with disgust. Then he
takes a deep breath. "Damn Hadley Addison! He's
right, you know; we couldn't handle the crowds." I can
see that it costs him a lot to say that. "But Cecilia's was
a fine place. I've got to keep it going somehow. . . ."

I've never seen him so defeated. My eyes feel
wet, too.

16

LORRAINE'S SOLUTION FOR DAD'S DEPRESSION WAS FOR them to get married immediately; that way, they'd have something to celebrate.

They rushed around to get a license and blood tests. Dad gave Lorraine a big bouquet of white lilacs, because that's her favorite flower, even though they're way out of season and not easy to find. She wore an ivory suit and Dad looked very handsome. The "for richer or poorer" part of the ceremony fit right in with the situation at Cecilia's.

Mona, a dancer friend of Lorraine's, stood up for her and I was best man. Having to wear a suit and tie wasn't all that bad.

Cecilia's is closed for the day, which isn't a big deal because hardly anyone's been coming in anyway. We pushed tables together to make one long one and we're having a feast. Dad and Cajun Jack worked on this one with demon energy, proving to the world that they are still the best and man, it is a triumph! Oysters Rockefeller, crayfish gumbo, chicken paprikasch Cecilia, wild rice, cucumber and dill salad, Dobos torte and pralines. Cajun Jack outdid himself with a towering white wedding cake topped with lilacs. The champagne is flowing freely and Maggie is very giggly and keeps hugging Bob, which seems to make him nervous.

Lorraine's friend Mona is exactly the kind of girl Dad used to go out with—blond and statuesque. She wears her good looks like a mask. Next to her, Lorraine is slim and delicate, her face wide open and vulnerable, big green-flecked hazel eyes full of light— and I can understand why Dad has changed his style in women. Dad is smiling and, for the first time this week, the strained look is gone.

Lorraine's parents flew in from Des Moines. They seem gentle and quiet, kind of Midwestern, and they look confused by Ellen's purple mascara and backless, sideless, and partly frontless dress. (It's great to see Ellen out of working clothes!) Actually, they seem confused by everything, but I think Dad has charmed them. They're younger than Grandma Van Dorn, but not nearly as straight backed and self-assured.

The tree twinkling in the corner reminds me that Christmas is almost here and I feel the guilt creeping in. After dessert, I slip upstairs and call her.

"Hi, Grandma. It's Andy."

"Well, Andrew. I'd hoped to hear from you. We don't want to trim the tree until you—"

"Grandma, I'm sorry, I—I'm not coming for Christmas. I haven't found my cat yet."

"Why should that interfere with—"

"I want to be home for Christmas. With Dad and . . ."

There's a pause and I don't know what to say.

"It's all right, Andrew. I'm disappointed, of course, but . . ." I hear a little intake of breath. "Of course. You want to be with your friends and . . . Well, I'll send your present. I don't know if it can arrive on time now. . . ."

"Grandma, I thought—if you could spend Christmas with us, here, that would be nice. I asked Dad and he said you're welcome." I did ask him; Dad doesn't hold grudges.

"I'm afraid I can't do that."

"I'd like it a lot if you'd come. If we were all together."

"No."

"It would be nice, Grandma. Morgan could drive you down for the day and—"

Her voice is steely. "I'm sorry, Andrew, I really can't. As a matter of fact, there's a function at the club."

"I'm sorry I disappointed you," I say. I hope there really is something at her club. I hate feeling so guilty.

"No, Andrew, it's all right. Well, I'll just send your present on, then. . . ."

I know it'll be something very expensive and much too preppy for me to wear. It doesn't matter. I love her.

"Thanks. I'll send your present, too, Grandma."

I wish she could unbend a little.

I can't find a way to tell her that Dad got married again. The funny thing is, I don't think my mother would mind. I think she'd like seeing Dad so happy. She might even like Lorraine.

"Well then, Andrew, I hope you'll visit soon."

"I will, Grandma."

I'll try to visit a lot more often. Maybe someday she'll want to be part of a family again, even if it's not the same one she started with.

"Merry Christmas, dear."

"Merry Christmas."

I'll go to the florist tomorrow. I'll order a rose-bush to be shipped in the spring and send the gift card to her now. A very tough winter-hardy rosebush. I think she'll like that.

Downstairs, Cajun Jack is making another toast, even though he sticks to club soda himself, and the mounds of whipped cream have melted into ooze. Through the frosted front windows, I can see snow beginning to fall. Maggie is at the point of singing a teary-eyed version of "Danny Boy" and Bob goes out to find a cab for her. Lorraine throws her bouquet to Ellen, who looks pleased, and everyone cheers. And then, when no one is looking, she tosses her potato to me. "I won't need this anymore," she says, radiant.

It's a little moldy, but I tuck it into my pocket. I need all the luck I can get. Christmas vacation hasn't started yet, so I still have to face school and Bear. And Katie has been gone for six days.

There've only been two calls about my lost cat notice. One was from someone who said, "Meow,

meow, meow," and hung up. I wonder what happens to people to make them get their kicks like that. The other was from a man who said he'd seen a big black cat with a red collar hanging around Morton Street for a couple of days. I ran over to Morton Street, thinking Katie's a small cat, but size is relative, and maybe she looks black in a certain light, even if she isn't, and she didn't have a collar, but maybe. . . . Halfway there, I knew it was hopeless, but I had to look anyway. I went up and down Morton Street, calling her. After a while, I saw a big black cat with a red collar. It wasn't Katie. Now it's snowing and I think we're running out of time.

It snowed all night and the next morning, the street sounds are muffled. It's still white when I leave for school and the outlines of buildings are softened. The scraggly tree outside our door is transformed into a Cinderella of frosting and sparkling icicles. There are piles of snow in alleys and on cellar stairs. By afternoon, it has turned to slush and crossing the streets becomes an exhibition of long jumping and wading.

Store decorations sparkle, people are scurrying about with bright packages, sidewalk Santas ring their bells, and the Salvation Army band's full-throated "Adeste Fidelis" sends holiday tidings down the block. All that cheer makes me even sadder.

I don't know how to think like a cat. Maybe my quiet-street theory is right, or maybe busy streets like Cecilia's would look familiar to her. Would she hide during the day and roam at night, or would she retain her old habits and do the opposite? Wherever I go, I automatically focus on hidden corners. I see lots of stray cats, looking miserable.

"Katie!" I call on my way home from school. "Katie!" I call as I go about my errands. If I keep this up, I'll become known as the Village idiot cat-boy.

Christmas comes and it's anticlimactic right after the wedding celebration. Cecilia's special Christmas dinner doesn't draw much of a crowd and Dad and Cajun Jack look worried again. We try hard to feel festive. Lorraine and Dad's gift for me is an electronic typewriter! That's pretty lavish, considering the cash register is not exactly overflowing. I have a feeling that was Lorraine's idea, her way of telling me to go for it. I roll in a sheet of paper, listen to the hum, tap on the keys, and feel like a pro. It's great. Maybe I'll be a journalist. I know I *don't* want to be a restaurant critic.

Then it's finally Christmas vacation—no more Miss Morfly, no more Bear Abbott, late late-night television, and mornings to sleep it off. I know I have to start giving up on Katie and do normal things again. Some cousins of Jo-Jo's are visiting for the holidays, so one day we take them to the South Street Seaport and look at the old ships and eat our way through the concessions. Another day, Orange and I hang out at the pizzeria and play video games. Kim O'Hara was there, in a booth with some other girls. I said "hi" and she said "hi" and that was all.

I'm getting used to the apartment being crowded. It worked out okay when Cajun Jack lived with us, so I guess it can hold three people. Anyway, Lorraine's so ecstatic that she manages to lift up everyone's mood. What happened is that she finally got a part in a new show. It's a musical comedy based on Franz Kafka's "The Metamorphosis." They're going to call it *Don't Bug Me.* Lorraine's one of the dancing cockroaches.

The streets are still too slushy for skateboarding, so a bunch of us go ice-skating in Central Park. We have fun but it's windy and after a while, it feels like subzero temperature. Wind chill factor, whatever that means. My toes and fingers get numb. The rented skates didn't fit right and my ankles are aching. I hobble home, smelling of wet wool, frozen through. I go upstairs and put on water for hot chocolate. I'm about to stir it when the telephone rings.

"Hello."

"Hello. Is this Cecilia's?" A woman's voice.

"Yes, it is."

"I'm calling about your lost cat." I can feel my heart jump. "I saw a cat that matched your description. Gray and black tabby?"

"Yes!"

"I saw her, not five minutes ago, in Washington Square Park. Just inside the park, the west side."

"The west side?" I think a happy ending is within reach!

"The uptown end. The northwest side."

"Thanks! Thanks a lot!"

"Well, I hope it's your cat."

I forget about being cold. I jump up and jam my feet into my Timberlands, leave them unlaced. I grab my jacket and zip it on the way out the door. I run, splashing in puddles, splattering slush. Five minutes ago! I run as fast as I can, one block, three blocks, a stitch in my side. Wait, Katie! Don't go anywhere.

I am panting hard when I reach the edge of the park. My eyes dart over the frozen ground. My throat is dry. I scan empty park benches. Then—ahead on the path—the maroon jacket of Bear Abbott, surrounded by a bunch of his friends, lounging against the railing! He's turned away from me, hasn't seen me yet. I stop for a split second. I could back up before he notices. I have time to get out of the park. But this is my chance to find Katie! I go forward, with fear a cold hand grabbing the back of my neck.

Bear spots me. I watch him unfurling himself from the railing. Then his bulk is directly in front of me, blocking my way.

"Go ahead, kid," he says. "Make my day."

He's doing his best steely eyed look, but he breaks it for a moment; he can't help smirking as he sees his friends lined up to watch. With an audience like that, I'm going to be pulverized. Then he's back to deadpan and gives my shoulder a hard shove as I try to keep moving.

He's going to make me lose Katie! Damn it, I can't lose Katie now!

"Okay, okay, get it over with," I say, frantic, my breath coming in gasps. "You want to beat me up, go ahead, do it, but do it fast, because I'm in a hurry!"

He shoves me again.

I'm full of rage and frustration. Katie! "C'mon, I'm not gonna fight back, we know you can cream me, so let's not waste *time*! You're not gonna kill me, right? You want to blacken my eyes? Okay, here, get it over with, just make it *fast,* damn it, and let me go!"

Through the blur in my eyes, I see Bear's stupidly puzzled expression. He's put off balance by the unexpected.

I can't keep my mouth shut. "Hurry up, punch me quick, come on, let's go!" I scream. "Beat me up, let's move it! Hurry up! Here, see, here's my eye, here's my nose. You wanna break it? I'm in a rush!"

"What is he, a retard or on something?" I hear one of Bear's cronies ask.

Bear shrugs.

"Come on, Abbott, the kid's a looney-tune," someone says.

I'm standing there with my hands down at my sides, ready to take whatever. "Make it *fast!* I'm running out of time!"

Miracle of miracles, Clint Eastwood doesn't know how to cope with a crazy! I'm not doing a thing for his status. He's undecided for a moment and then he saves face by muttering, "You're lucky I'm not in a punching mood," and he *lets me go!*

"Katie!" I call. I walk up and down the paths. "Katie!" I see them watching me, so every once in a while, I flap my arms and add a little tap dance. "Katie!" No sign of a cat.

I go under the Arch and along the NYU side. "Katie!" I cover the entire park. It gets dark and I circle the surrounding blocks. "Katie!" And finally, I have to give up. She could have gone miles in any direction by now. Or it could have been another tabby. I'll never know.

There's nothing more to do but go home. My cheeks are stinging from the cold. My eyes are stinging, too. I go past bus shelters and stores and see that a lot of my notices are missing. Katie has been gone for twelve days. I'd accept never seeing her again if I could believe that someone took her in. The truth is, she's a perfectly ordinary-looking cat. Her chances aren't too good.

Someday I'll take in a stray. I couldn't now, but someday. Kind of in her memory. There's something Dad said to me the night before the wedding. "Andy," he said, "don't think this means I've forgotten your mother. I loved her more than I can say—and that makes me open to loving again." I think I understand.

I'm already on Cecilia's corner when the thought hits me. I stood up to Bear! In a peculiar way, maybe, but I didn't back off. I didn't know he would let me go, so . . . you might call that brave. I guess no one's brave one hundred percent of the time. I can come through when the stakes are high. Maybe I'm a lot more like Dad than I thought. I'm feeling good about myself.

The real test of my freedom from Bear comes when school starts again. On the first day back, I pass him in the halls. There's a crowd, perfect for a Bear Abbott exhibition. I see his eyes flick over me for signs of mania. Then he tests the water with his usual threats.

"Voodoo parsnips!" I shout at him. "Blue cow!" I jab my finger in the air. "Watch the flypaper! Moo. Moo."

Bear's features form into a kind of stupid wariness and he moves on. Around the corner, I double over, laughing. I guess no one wants to get enmeshed with unpredictable insanity. The mad umbrella lady of West Forty-fourth Street was right!

17

A FUNNY THING HAPPENED TO CECILIA'S ON THE WAY TO oblivion.

The way I heard it, on that night when Herb Lee was so depressed, he went back across the street to do his second show. His material fell flatter than ever and he was being tortured by hecklers, and he decided to quit show business. He was so miserable and angry that he didn't care anymore.

"You don't have to stick around till the end of my spot," he told his tormentors. "Go across the street. Have dinner at Cecilia's instead. Enjoy some catfish in your goulash. . . ."

And from there, he went into a wildly exaggerated improvisation on all the troubles we'd had, complete with impersonations of Ellen and Cajun Jack. Just out of sheer indifference, he became funnier and funnier. His act was a smash and, after a couple of weeks, he wound up booked into Catch a Rising Star and somebody important saw him there, and then the next thing we knew, he was starring on TV. By spring, he was up for a movie with Eddie Murphy and there's another one in the works, based on the Cecilia's routine, with Herb as the owner in a hot romance with Dolly Parton as the waitress. (Ellen was out of joint about not being asked to play herself and Lorraine feels it should be a musical with a part for a dancer.)

Now Cecilia's is known as Herb Lee's hangout. The celebrity watchers who came sampled the food and enjoyed it and came back for more. We've got a big crowd coming in, but Dad and Cajun Jack have learned from experience. It's all strictly by reservation and we don't try to serve more than we can handle. That makes it seem exclusive and a reservation at Cecilia's has become a status symbol.

The other thing that happened puts the news about Herb Lee and Cecilia's in the shade.

Back during that bleak, slushy January, I came home from school on the kind of day when it gets dark too early and the chill eats right through your bones. I was late because I'd been working on the school newspaper and I was tired and hungry. I was at the front door, when I heard a meow. I thought my imagination was playing tricks again, but then there was a whole string of them, "meow, meow, meow," frantic, one on top of the other. A cat ran to my feet from under a parked car and in the dark, I could just make out stripes. Stripes! Katie!

I gathered her up and she was weightless, a phantom cat. Inside the lighted restaurant, I saw the protruding bones and the hard, matted fur. Her eyes were huge and haunted and her head was out of proportion with the thin body. But Katie, half-starved and exhausted, had made it home!

Today it's many saucers of milk, much cat food, months of brushings and purrings later. Katie is sleeping in my lap and she sighs with deep contentment. Everything is right in the world of Andy Szabo—but life is unpredictable. New things keep popping up and you never know if they'll turn out good or bad or somewhere in between. For instance—the phone rings.

"Hello," I say, in my usual original way.

"Hi, Andy. This is Kim O'Hara."

Gulp. I haven't seen the beauteous O'Hara since school let out for the summer.

"I was just wondering . . . remember when we were talking, a while ago, you said you wanted your ear pierced?"

"Uh-huh," I say.

"Did you ever get it done?"

"Uh—no," I say wittily.

"Well, I was just thinking. I'm not doing anything right now, so if you maybe wanted to come over, I'd do it for you. . . ."

"Yeah, sure. Great! I'll be right there, Kim!"

So now I'm booking down the street straight to Kim O'Hara's house in a miasma of confusion! Does this mean she likes me or was she just seized with sudden bloodlust? And if she likes me, how do I act?

Do I ask her to go out right away or wait or what? And if that turns out all right, what if my earlobe gets infected? And even if it doesn't, Dad is old-fashioned macho. He's going to *kill* if he ever sees me with an earring! But Kim O'Hara's worth it . . . and I'm almost there.

    And it's
        never
            really

The End